"I told you when we split up that I would always be here if you needed me for anything. That hasn't changed."

Lisa had never expected to take Wade up on that offer. She had left North Carolina determined to prove to him, to her father, to everyone that she was perfectly capable of taking care of herself.

It had meant walking away from the man she had loved with the full intensity of her younger heart, but somehow she had done it.

"Thank you, Wade," she said, knowing he was sincere in his concern for her. "But the_____ny momentary meltdown ea____

"I'm sure you can. But I ____

"I'm always open to sug____

"You can move in with me."

Dear Reader,

Some ten years ago, my now-eighteen-year-old son was given a remote control, rainbow-colored race car, and it quickly became one of his favorite toys. Soon afterward, he happened to find a race taking place on television—and he was thrilled to see that same car speeding around the track. *His* car, he said excitedly, urging me to sit down and watch with him. We watched the colorful car win the race and the handsome young racer climb out and celebrate with his crew—and this romance writer with a fondness for larger-than-life heroes was hooked immediately.

The addictive sport soon drew in my son's two older sisters, both of whom quickly chose their own favorite drivers. The thrill of competition, the excitement and color of the events, but most of all the diversity of the personalities involved all combined to make us a family of rabid NASCAR fans. We've spent countless Sunday afternoons in front of the TV, cheering on the drivers we like (because we all have several favorites), getting to "know" the announcers and owners and crew chiefs and other NASCAR notables, feeling in some small way like a part of the larger NASCAR family.

That's why it was such a thrill for me to be invited to participate in this exciting series of NASCAR romances. The possibilities within this fascinating sport are endless—and I'm so excited to be bringing two stories to you about two dashing NASCAR heroes and the strong women who fall in love with them. I hope you enjoy reading them as much as I've had fun writing them.

Gina Wilkins

NASCAR

HEARTS UNDER CAUTION

Gina Wilkins

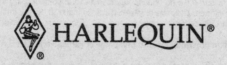

HARLEQUIN®

TORONTO • NEW YORK • LONDON
AMSTERDAM • PARIS • SYDNEY • HAMBURG
STOCKHOLM • ATHENS • TOKYO • MILAN • MADRID
PRAGUE • WARSAW • BUDAPEST • AUCKLAND

ISBN-13: 978-0-373-21768-7
ISBN-10:   0-373-21768-4

HEARTS UNDER CAUTION

GINA WILKINS

Bestselling romance author Gina Wilkins has written more than eighty novels for Harlequin and Silhouette Books, yet she still finds excitement in every new idea. A lifelong resident of Arkansas, she is a four-time winner of the prestigious Maggie Award for Excellence presented by Georgia Romance Writers and has won several awards from *Romantic Times BOOKreviews,* including a nomination for a Lifetime Achievement Award. She credits her enduring career in romance to her long-suffering husband and her three "extraordinary" children, all of whom have provided inspiration over the years.

For my family, John, Courtney, Kerry and David.
Here's to many more lazy Sunday afternoons together.

CHAPTER ONE

THE MOONLIT NIGHT WAS STILL, the late July temperature warm but comfortable as Lisa Woodrow sat on a concrete bench in her mother's North Carolina garden. Heavy perfumes from many varieties of roses tickled her nose and carried her back to her past. As she had so often in those blissfully naive and hopelessly romantic younger days, she found herself thinking of Wade McClellan....

A rustling in a far corner of the large garden brought her abruptly back to the present. Every nerve ending in her body on sudden alert, she sat up straight, straining her ears. When the sound wasn't repeated, she let out the breath she'd been holding and tried to relax, assuring herself that there was nothing to fear here.

She had plenty of reason to be on edge after the events of the past week. It didn't soothe her frazzled nerves to know that Wade was inside her parents' house, meeting with her father and a few other top members of the Woodrow Racing team.

Since team owner Ernest "Woody" Woodrow had undergone a full hip replacement ten days earlier, limiting his movements for a few weeks, the majority of his meetings had taken place here, in his home office.

His highest-ranking team members had arrived right after dinner on this Monday evening to discuss the race week ahead. Wade had been the first of those arrivals.

It had been obvious that he hadn't known Lisa was there, since she'd flown in only a few hours earlier, but he had recovered quickly from his surprise. He'd greeted her with the same polite distance he'd displayed on the few other occasions when they'd crossed paths over the last six years. She'd responded in the same cool manner—and had made her escape at the very first available opportunity.

It was the first time she'd seen him in over a year. He looked tired, she thought. Too thin. His tanned skin was drawn a little too tightly over the carved planes of his face. His brown eyes were shadowed, the sun-creases at the corners more deeply defined than she remembered. And there was now a touch of gray at the temples of his functionally short, pecan-brown hair.

Yet even as she acknowledged the signs that he hadn't changed his fiercely workaholic habits, her heart pounded so hard in her chest that she'd been afraid he could hear it over her cool, carefully disinterested voice. After almost six years and a whole new life, one would think she'd have gotten over the sight of him by now.

The rustling came again.

It brought Lisa to her feet. Poised for flight, she held her breath, trying to hear over her hammering pulse. She'd thought the sound came from behind her and to the left, but was she wrong? Had it been between her and the safety of the house?

No. Definitely behind her.

Maybe it was a cat, or some other small, nocturnal animal. Maybe nothing but overwrought imagination. She didn't stick around to find out. She bolted, heading straight for the house, making no effort to be quiet.

When she slammed into a solid and unmistakably male body, she reacted on pure instinct, striking out. She opened her mouth to scream.

"Lisa!" Wade's voice cut through her moment of panic, turning the budding shriek into a squeak of surprise. His hands fell on her shoulders, steadying them both and making her realize how close she'd come to flattening him. "What's wrong? Are you okay?"

Her breath was still coming out too audibly, a combination of her former fear and now awareness of Wade standing so close to her, holding her. She took a quick step backward, dislodging his hands.

He let his arms fall to his sides, but his too-sharp gaze remained on her face. "What's wrong?" he repeated.

She took a moment to regain control. She could barely see him in the diffused garden lighting, but she knew her own face was more visible to him since there was a pole lamp directly behind him, illuminating her while keeping him in the shadows.

"I thought I heard someone moving around in the garden," she said when she was sure her voice would come out relatively steady. "Watching me."

His head lifted as if he'd just caught scent of a predator. Looking from side to side, he asked, "Where?"

She started to point in the direction she'd thought the noise had come from, but then stopped and shook her head. "I'm not sure. If anyone was there, he'd be gone by now anyway."

"You know it's unlikely anyone was in the garden with you. The property is fully fenced and your dad has top of the line security equipment. It wouldn't be easy for anyone to get in nor to get back out unnoticed."

"Yes, I know." But the hesitancy she heard in her response probably let him know she wasn't entirely re-assured. To distract him, she asked, "What are you doing out here? Were you looking for me?"

"Yeah. I was."

Even though she had asked, his answer still surprised her. "Why?"

"I got the impression that something was bothering you. Something more than me being here, I mean. I wanted to see if there's anything I can do."

She supposed she shouldn't be so taken aback that he'd seen too much during their brief interaction earlier. Wade had always read her too well—with a few very painful exceptions. "I'm okay."

"Are you sure? Because you look kind of shaky."

What pride she retained after being caught by Wade on the verge of a full-blown panic attack kicked into full force. She lifted her chin. "I'm fine, Wade. I guess I'm just tired. It's my first real vacation in almost three years. I hadn't realized quite how much I needed one. Now, if you'll excuse me, I think I'll head inside, maybe turn in early tonight."

"Lisa—"

Ignoring the hand he held out to detain her, she

stepped around him and moved resolutely toward her parents' house. "Good night, Wade," she said over her shoulder without looking back.

It was no surprise that he didn't respond.

WADE WAS BACK THE NEXT MORNING. Lisa hadn't seen him when he arrived, but her mother told her that he was meeting with Woody and the other three Woodrow Racing crew chiefs in Woody's office. Sitting in the solarium before noon, surrounded by her mother's pampered and beloved flowering plants, Lisa merely shrugged when her mother asked her how she felt about Wade being around so much during her visit.

"He isn't usually here at the house," Ellen added a bit anxiously. "You know, your father usually prefers not to do business at home. But since his surgery, it's easier for the meetings to be held here."

"I understand—and it's fine, Mom. I certainly don't want to interfere with Dad's business meetings just because I'm here for a visit. And as for Wade, you know he and I have seen each other several times during the past few years. It's not a problem."

"It can't be comfortable for you, having your ex-fiancé in the house," Ellen fretted.

Smiling, Lisa shook her head. "It's not a problem," she repeated. "My ex-fiancé still works for my father. It's a given that he and I will run into each other at times. Besides, it isn't as if Wade and I had a bitter breakup. It was all very amicable, remember? We've remained friendly."

She didn't go so far as to say they were still friends. She wasn't sure she and Wade had ever been friends, even when they were lovers. He hadn't let her get to know him that well.

Virginia Cooper, who had been employed by the family since Lisa was barely out of diapers, appeared in the doorway with a smile to announce that lunch was ready. There had been a time when Virginia had only worked a couple of days a week doing the laundry and the heavy cleaning, but since Ellen had taken ill a year ago, she came in every day to cook and run the household.

Ellen had protested at first, but Lisa suspected that she was secretly grateful for the extra help. Now she spent her days caring for her flowers, fussing over her husband and resting quite a bit.

Lisa's steps faltered a little when she saw Wade waiting with her father in the breakfast nook where the informal luncheon was to be served. He gave her a rather stiff nod of greeting.

"Wade and I aren't quite through with our business today," Woody announced gruffly. "He's going to be joining us for lunch and then we'll finish up afterward. I'm sure that's okay with you ladies?"

Though he'd posed it as a question, it was obvious that Woody expected no protests from his wife or daughter. It wasn't that he was oblivious to the awkwardness inherent in the situation, Lisa thought in resignation. It was just that he didn't have time for old dramas when he had business to discuss.

As much as he cared for his family, business always

came first for her father. It was a fact Lisa had accepted a very long time ago.

As was their usual habit, her parents sat at opposite ends of the small breakfast table, so that Lisa and Wade faced each other from the sides. Ellen didn't believe in long, stilted silences at her table, so she kicked off the conversation as they began to eat the cold chicken salad, fresh asparagus spears and fruit compote that Virginia had served for a light lunch.

"How have you been, Wade?" she asked cordially. "Have you fully recovered from that flu bug you picked up a few weeks ago?"

So that was why he still looked a bit worn, Lisa thought, glancing at the lines around his mouth. She didn't remember Wade ever being sick when she was involved with him; he said he didn't have time to deal with germs.

"Yes, ma'am, I'm feeling fine now," he said with the same deference he had always displayed toward his boss's wife. "Thank you for asking."

"Took him down pretty hard," Woody said to Lisa. "He missed three days of work that week. Made it to the racetrack, though."

"Of course he did," she murmured without looking at Wade. He'd have to be on his deathbed to miss a race, she thought. And she wouldn't guarantee even then that he wouldn't take the risk of just dropping dead in the pits, doing what he loved more than anything—or anyone—in the world.

"Lisa, do you have any interesting stories to tell us

about your job in Chicago?" her mother asked determinedly. "Any exciting cases lately?"

Other than the case that had sent her running to North Carolina out of fear for her very life? "Not really," she said with a bland smile. "Just the usual."

She sensed Wade's intense gaze on her face. It took an effort for her to keep her smile intact.

"Your mother got all nervous last week because she decided your life was just like one of those mystery novels she's always reading," Woody said with an indulgent shake of his head.

Looking a little sheepish, Ellen smiled. "I was reading a story about a prosecutor who was stalked by the vengeful relative of a criminal she'd put away," she explained. "It was set in L.A., but I couldn't help but think about you. Chicago is such a dangerous city and you deal with so many unsavory people in your job."

Lisa felt the corners of her smile tremble, but she forced her lips to behave. "Chicago's not as bad as you make it sound, Mom. And my life really isn't all that dramatic."

She wasn't exactly lying, she assured herself. Her job usually wasn't dangerous. But how coincidental was it that her mother had read that book so recently? Just talking about it made the color fade from her mom's face.

She shouldn't have come here, Lisa thought guiltily. She should have taken her boss's suggestion to find someplace safe and secluded to vacation for a few weeks, keeping her problems far away from her parents, who had enough to worry about right now. But for some reason she'd found herself wanting to come home, even though she had promised herself she wouldn't tell her family the real purpose behind the extended visit.

Obviously, she hadn't thought her decision through. She certainly hadn't planned to be lunching with Wade only a day after her arrival.

"You must be really excited about the way this season is going," she said brightly to her father, hoping no one would see any significance in the jarringly sudden change of topic. "Two of your drivers sitting in the top ten points positions and a third driver not far behind. That would really be something if three of your four teams ended up in The Chase at the end, wouldn't it?"

Both her dad and Wade looked at her oddly, as if they were surprised that she knew where the Woodrow Racing drivers stood in points coming up on the twentieth race of the thirty-sixth race season. Maybe they were startled that she even knew that only the top ten points leaders and those drivers within 400 points of first place were eligible to race for the NASCAR NEXTEL Cup during the last ten races of the season, a system referred to as The Chase for the Championship.

She supposed she shouldn't be surprised by *their* surprise. Since her father had been so determined to keep his family and work life separate, she had been kept well away from the racing world in her youth, forced to learn about the sport by watching televised race coverage like the average fan.

"Er, yeah," Woody said awkwardly. "We're doing real good."

"Mom said you and Wade have been meeting about hiring a new engineer. How's the search going?"

"Good," her father said with a curt nod. "Got it narrowed down to just a few. We'll talk about it some more after lunch. This salad's good, Virginia. I like the almonds in it."

Having just approached the table with a pitcher of iced tea to refill their glasses, the housekeeper beamed. "I'm glad you like it, Mr. Woody. Does anyone need anything else before I go?"

When everyone assured her that nothing else was needed, Virginia told them to enjoy their meals and to leave their dishes when they were finished. She bustled away to finish her chores, leaving a silence in her wake that even Ellen didn't seem to know how to fill as they finished their lunches.

Wade finished his business with Woody an hour and a half after they'd returned to Woody's office after lunch. Leaving Woody already engrossed in a conference call with a potential sponsor, he made his way through the house toward the front door, needing no escort.

The house was quiet; he suspected that Ellen was napping, as was her habit in the afternoons since she'd been ill. He didn't know where Lisa was—not that he was looking, he assured himself.

He had his answer when he passed the open doorway of the front salon, just off the entryway. It was a room the family used as a library. Lisa was inside, her back turned toward him as she stood in front of a filled bookcase, looking through her mother's treasured collection of mystery novels.

Wade paused, considered moving on without speaking but then changed his mind. He was suddenly reminded of the conversation they'd had at lunch, when Ellen had told them about the book she'd recently read. Something about a prosecutor being targeted by a killer. Ellen had looked sheepish about taking the tale too seriously and being worried for her daughter's sake. But it was Lisa's expression he remembered most vividly.

She hadn't laughed off her mother's concerns. She had made some offhand remark about not confusing fact with fiction—but then she'd quickly changed the subject. And he would have sworn she'd lost a couple of shades of color from her face—which had already been pale.

He had suspected since he'd first seen her yesterday that something was going on with Lisa. Something she wasn't telling her family. And even though it was absolutely none of his business, he couldn't help but feel that he should offer his assistance, if she needed it. Though he doubted there was anything he could do for her—or that she would accept his help, regardless.

Making a sudden decision, he moved forward. "Lisa?"

She gasped and jumped half a foot, whirling around as if she'd heard a gun cock behind her.

"Oh," she said, her voice unsteady. "Wade. You startled me."

"Sorry." He studied her face, convinced now that

he'd been right about something shady going on with her. "What's up?"

"I was just looking for something to read."

He shook his head impatiently. "You've taken a month's vacation from your job. You've lost weight. You jump halfway out of your shoes at the slightest sound. Maybe your mother accepts your explanation that you've just been working too hard and need a break, but that doesn't cut it with me. Your dad thinks there's more to it, too."

"Sounds like my father's been talking too much," she grumbled.

"He's worried about you. He thinks the job's too much for you to handle."

"My father can't understand why I'd want to be a prosecutor when I could stay here and let him take care of me. Or find some other man to take care of me," she added a bit pointedly. "But I love my job. And I am quite capable of handling it just fine, thank you."

"I never doubted it," Wade muttered, hearing the resignation in his own voice. "But you're sure there isn't something bothering you? Nothing I can do to help? Even if it's just to serve as a sounding board. I'm available now for a couple of hours."

She looked ready to brush him off again. But then she bit her lip, looked toward the doorway and nervously tucked a lock of her straight blond hair behind her ear.

"Lees?" he said more gently, using her old nickname for the first time in almost six years. "Let me help."

She sighed deeply. "I shouldn't have come here. I

thought it would be safe for a few weeks and that my parents would be safe with me here. Now…now I'm questioning the wisdom of that decision."

"Okay, now you're just creeping me out," he said bluntly, reaching out to lay his hand on her shoulder. "Tell me what's going on."

"It's going to take a while," she said after another long pause. "And I'd rather my parents didn't hear what I have to say. Not yet, anyway."

He nodded, both relieved that she seemed willing to talk and unnerved by what little she had already said. "Then we need to go where we can talk in private. Want to have a drink with me somewhere?"

She hesitated only another moment, then nodded. "Yes. To be honest, I would be grateful for your advice."

Though he was a bit surprised that she'd accepted his invitation, he didn't let it show. Over the past few years he'd gotten very good at hiding his emotions from Lisa, he thought wryly. Just as he did from everyone else.

THE COFFEE SHOP WADE TOOK HER to was small. Quiet on a Tuesday afternoon. Sitting in a cozy booth at the back with Lisa, Wade knew he'd been recognized by some of the other customers, but they gave him his privacy. Perhaps they sensed that he was in no mood for socializing.

Her parents had been startled, to say the least, when Lisa had told them that she and Wade were going out for a while. It had been obvious that they hadn't expected her to spend any time alone with her ex-fiancé during her visit. And just as obvious that her mother wasn't overly enthusiastic about her doing so today.

Wade couldn't say he thought this was a brilliant idea, either. He didn't want to be reminded of those earlier days with Lisa, nor of the painful end to their relationship. But he still remembered all too clearly the look on her face when she'd run straight into his arms in her mother's garden last night. Not to mention the way she'd jumped when he'd simply said her name in the library.

Something was seriously wrong in her life. He had looked into her smoky green eyes and had seen something he'd never seen in Lisa Woodrow before. Fear.

Because it was late in the afternoon, Lisa ordered a decaf latte. Wade ordered coffee. Black and real. He was usually too tired by the time he crawled into bed for caffeine to keep him awake, no matter how much he consumed during the day.

"Now tell me what's going on," he said when they had their drinks in front of them.

He hadn't meant the request to sound so much like a command. He blamed his curt tone on his uneasiness about her, but he knew Lisa didn't respond well to being given orders. Especially from him. He tried to soften his expression. "Please."

Predictably, she had bristled a little but he'd managed to appease her. She nodded, tucked a lock of hair behind her ear, then gazed into her coffee mug for a moment before saying, "I might have made a mistake coming here."

"Here? With me? Or here, to your parents' house?"

"Both," she said, making a face. "But specifically, I was talking about my parents' house."

As a crew chief, Wade was often forced to hide his feelings. No matter how bad things got during a race, he had to stay upbeat and optimistic, keeping his driver and team calm and focused, making them all believe he had everything under control. His owner, the sponsors, the media, the fans—no one could tell by his demeanor when things weren't going well with the team. When he was worried or discouraged or stressed.

They called him "Ice." A nickname he tolerated because he'd worked hard to earn it.

Never was he more hard-pressed to hide his feelings than when he was around Lisa. Even after six years, all it took was a little wrinkle of her nose to make his heart stutter. Damn, she was even more beautiful now than she'd been as the girl who had once loved him.

"Maybe you'd better start from the beginning," he said, and this time he didn't care if he sounded too bossy. It was better than letting her see that she still affected him entirely too deeply.

"I know you think I'm home on vacation. But actually, I took a leave of absence because my boss insisted on it," she admitted grudgingly. "And I came home to North Carolina because it was either that or go into protective custody back in Chicago. You see, someone there is trying to kill me."

CHAPTER TWO

LISA COULD TELL THAT SHE HAD taken Wade completely off guard. Maybe he'd been expecting her to tell him some tale about a romance gone bad. This was much worse.

She still wasn't sure what had convinced her to confide in him. Maybe she just needed someone to talk to—and he had been available. More likely, it was her confidence that if anyone here could help her, it would be Wade.

As her father's long-time employee, and the crew chief for up-and-coming driver Jake Hinson, Wade was accustomed to solving problems, putting out fires even before they started. Who better to give her a candid opinion about the wisdom of the course she had chosen and to offer suggestions to make sure neither she—nor anyone she loved—suffered from that choice?

"I successfully prosecuted a drug dealer last month. A real bad guy, Jesse Norris; they've been after him for years. He made some threats, both to my face and through others, blustered a lot, but I didn't let him rattle me. He got sent away. And then he escaped."

"Escaped?"

She nodded. "He was being transported to prison and he managed to get away somehow. Everyone believes he had help. He's been on the loose for almost three weeks. Since then I've received two threats by mail, untraceable so far. Two weeks ago the judge in the case was almost killed by a crude, homemade explosive device. A few days later someone took a shot at the jury foreman. And this past weekend someone tried to break into my apartment."

Wade's brown eyes narrowed to glittering slits in his lean, tanned face. "Were you at home?"

"Yes." She swallowed, remembering the way she'd felt when she'd heard someone at her window in the middle of the night. "Fortunately, I was awake when I heard the faint sounds, so I wasn't taken by surprise in my sleep."

She'd been lying in her bed thinking about Wade, actually. She had seen his driver, Jake Hinson, in a television interview for a racing program that day, and the thought of Wade had haunted her all evening. No way, of course, would she tell him that now—or ever, for that matter.

His face seemed to have tightened when he asked, "What did you do?"

"I dialed 9-1-1 and shouted that I was doing so. I also said that I had a gun and that it was pointed at the window. Whoever it was had gone by the time the police arrived."

Wade let out a long, deep breath. "Did you have a gun?"

She leveled a look at him. "I'm Woody Woodrow's daughter. Of course I had a gun. It's registered."

The faintest hint of a smile quirked the corner of his

mouth but it disappeared almost immediately. "So you came here."

"My boss insisted I take a month off. Actually, he wanted me in protective custody, but when I convinced him that my father's security is as good as any I could have found in Chicago, he gave in. I haven't had a vacation in a couple of years and I was due, even though this is hardly the way I would choose to spend it. Now…well, I'm wondering if I should have stayed in Chicago."

"Why?"

"It truly didn't occur to me that anyone might follow me here. Not until I thought I heard someone moving around in the garden last night. There was probably no one there, but it made me think. My mother isn't in good health, you know that. And Dad—well, he'd go ballistic if he found out about all this."

Wade winced. "That's an understatement."

"So, I should go back to Chicago? Or somewhere else where I can hole up quietly until Norris is recaptured? It shouldn't be that much longer. I mean, he's not exactly lying low."

"I don't like the thought of you going off somewhere yourself. And to be honest, I don't have a lot of faith in standard protective custody."

"I won't put my parents at risk. And I don't want to burden them with this. I shouldn't have even said anything to you, but…well, you caught me at a vulnerable moment. I guess I just needed to talk to someone."

Wade met her gaze levelly. "I told you when we split

up that I would always be here if you needed me for anything. That hasn't changed."

She had never expected to take him up on that offer. She had left North Carolina determined to prove to him, to her father, to everyone that she was perfectly capable of taking care of herself. That she didn't need a man to shelter her and protect her and support her—while at the same time ignoring her for the sake of his all-consuming career. Maybe her mother had been content to live that way, but Lisa had come to the sudden realization—six months before her wedding—that she couldn't do it.

It had meant walking away from the man she had loved with the full intensity of her young heart, but somehow she had done it. And as much as she had grieved for that lost love, as often as she dreamed of him to this day, she did not regret the choice she had made.

"Thank you, Wade," she said, knowing he was sincere in his concern for her. "But there's really nothing you can do. Despite my momentary meltdown earlier, I can handle this."

"I'm sure you can. But I do have a suggestion."

"I'm always open to suggestions."

He set his coffee cup down on the table, cupped both hands around it and looked at her without expression. "You can move in with me."

HER FIRST INSTINCT WAS TO TELL HIM he was out of his mind. Well, actually, that was her second reaction, she had to admit, if only to herself. Her first was a deep, unwelcome thrill of excitement at the very thought of moving in with Wade. "That's not an option."

He shook his head impatiently, looking as if he had expected that response. "Hear me out, Lees. It isn't what it sounds like."

Lees. Until this afternoon, he hadn't called her that since the night she'd told him she didn't want to marry him. And that she had been accepted into law school without even telling him she had applied.

"I don't understand."

"You *could* stay in my house here, but I'll be gone a lot during the next few weeks and you'd be by yourself there. So that's not an option. Besides, your folks wouldn't understand why you'd rather stay in my house than theirs while you're visiting here. I'm thinking you could travel with the team, staying in my motor home at the tracks. You'd be surrounded by people at all times and you'd be protected by the security staff."

For an off-the-cuff idea, it wasn't bad. But then, that was what Wade was best at, making and revising plans quickly and as needed. Which didn't necessarily mean she should go along with this one.

"I don't know, Wade…"

"Would you rather stay locked in a little dive somewhere, trusting the cops to keep an eye on you during the occasional drive-by surveillance? Or sit in your parents' house trying to keep your situation a secret while hoping that nothing happens to put them at risk?"

That was something else she knew about Wade—he had never learned to tactfully mince words.

"No," she said, equally candid. "I don't particularly like either of those options. But I don't think traveling with you is any smarter."

"I'm not suggesting anything more than a plan to keep you safe," he assured her. "I'll bunk with Jake or in someone's motel room, if necessary. I'll be so busy at the tracks that you'll hardly even see me."

She didn't doubt that. During racing season, she'd barely seen him even when they were engaged. Even during off-season he'd spent nineteen of every twenty-four hours thinking, planning, talking and living for racing. Which, when figuring in another four hours or so for sleeping, only left about an hour a day for him to focus on her.

"What would we tell everyone?" she asked, intrigued despite herself.

He shrugged. "The most believable cover story would be that we're making a stab at getting back together. After a couple of weeks, when this Norris guy has been recaptured, we'll let everyone believe I screwed it up again and we'll go back to being civil acquaintances. You can tell your folks the truth then, or you can leave them in innocent bliss. Whichever you think they can handle."

It didn't escape her that he'd taken the blame for their breakup. She didn't know whether he truly believed that or was getting in a little dig—something else she wouldn't put past Wade. She supposed it didn't really matter. She certainly wasn't getting into any discussions about what had gone wrong between them six years ago.

"It sounds awkward."

He nodded. "Yeah. But you've gotta admit it beats some of the other options."

She bit her lip for a moment, then asked, "Where's the race this week?"

"We'll be in Pennsylvania."

She had never been to that racetrack, since neither her father nor Wade had encouraged her to travel with the team. They'd told her the crowds were too big and the garage action too hectic. Her dad had said he didn't want to call undue attention to his only child, for security purposes.

What they had both implied was that she would be in their way.

Wade had actually told her once that she interfered with the intense concentration he required on race weekends. And he hadn't even been a crew chief then, but a car chief, obviously on the fast track to the top. So she had watched the races on television with her mother, who rarely made an appearance at the tracks.

"You're sure I won't interfere with your concentration?"

A muscle twitched in his jaw, the only indication that he recalled the conversation she had alluded to. "I've learned to block out distractions. I'm not quite as obsessive about my routines as I used to be."

Was he saying that he had changed? She didn't believe that for a minute. He wasn't aware, of course, that she'd been privately following his career since they'd broken up. He hadn't gotten to where he was, hadn't brought the team to where it was, without the same total dedication and commitment he'd always given to his career.

It was rather ironic that there were people who'd accused her of being the same way about *her* job.

"All right," she said, hoping she wasn't making a huge mistake. "If you're sure it won't be too much of an inconvenience for you, I'll take you up on that offer. I'd rather not have to worry my parents with this right now. Traveling with you and the team makes a good cover, actually—and like you said, there's safety in numbers."

He nodded. "I can step up security around you at the track without tipping off your folks. We'll leave Thursday afternoon for Pennsylvania. In the meantime, hang close to your parents' house and I'll be around to see you when I can, which will make it more believable when you leave with me Thursday. And if I were you, I wouldn't be sitting outside by myself at night."

She started to take offense at his autocratic tone, even opened her mouth to remind him that she wasn't a member of his crew who took orders from him without question—but then she reminded herself that he was doing her a big favor. He was taking time out of his precious schedule to help her out and that was a major concession from Wade.

"Why are you doing this?" she asked instead.

He hesitated only a moment before replying. "Because I'm concerned about your mother," he said finally. "Her health has been kind of precarious lately. I know your dad's been worried about her. If she found out about the threats against you, I'm afraid it would be too much for her. As for your father, he's got enough to worry about. I've been telling him he needs to cut back some and he doesn't need another problem added to his plate."

She didn't like being seen as a health hazard to her mother and another worrisome problem for her father. She almost wished now that she hadn't told Wade about her situation. That she hadn't come to North Carolina at all. She could have taken a long vacation somewhere quiet, safe and private, without anyone here having any idea that the career she'd left to pursue had led her into this kind of trouble.

"I'll try not to give them any reason to worry," she muttered.

"They'll worry that you're getting involved with me again," he said with a wry smile. "But at least they won't be concerned that you're in any physical danger."

His smile set off a cascade of emotions inside her. No, she didn't have to worry too much about physical danger if she went along with this impromptu plan. But maybe she should be a lot more concerned about the danger to the heart she'd thought she'd protected a long time ago from Wade McClellan.

"I DON'T LIKE THIS, LISA. Don't like it at all."

Lisa looked across the kitchen table Wednesday morning at her father's scowling face. She had to remind herself that she wasn't a little girl anymore, desperate to win her difficult father's attention and approval.

A big man with a booming voice and a fierce drive to succeed, Ernest Woodrow had made his fortune from multiple car dealerships and a chain of auto accessories stores started by his father. Through single-minded determination and twenty-four/seven concentration, Woody had doubled his inheritance by the time he was forty and had invested in his first race team. Now, at sixty, he ran four cars full-time in NASCAR NEXTEL Cup racing and had at least one driver on the fast track to a championship.

His success had come at a price to his family. The confirmed workaholic firmly believed that "his women" were to be sheltered and protected, indulged in anything they wanted materially, but otherwise were to be pretty much ignored. Lisa had no doubt now that he loved her and her mother but she hadn't been so confident of that when she'd been young and insecure.

It was when she had realized that she and Wade had been falling into the same patterns as her parents that she'd started to consider breaking off their engagement. She'd known she was too much like her father to be content for long in trying to live like her mother.

Lisa had to put that memory behind her when she said, "But, Daddy, I thought you would be pleased that Wade and I are spending time together again."

Her father had, after all, approved of the engagement—once he'd gotten over his resistance to his innocent little girl dating a man five years her senior. After some consideration, Lisa assumed he'd decided that it would be nice to keep the business in the family.

Since he didn't have a son to pass his interests to—and couldn't imagine a woman, even his own daughter, taking over his team—it made perfect sense to him for Lisa to marry a man with racing in his blood.

He had not at all approved of her decision to break off the engagement and enter law school. And when he'd found out that she intended to be a criminal prose-cutor rather than specializing in softer areas of the law—prenuptial agreements and high-profile divorces—he'd, well, blown a gasket, to use the jargon of his avocation.

He shook his balding head. "It's not that I mind you seeing him again. Never understood why you broke up with him in the first place. I hope you are coming to your senses about that job of yours. Dealing with criminals and murderers all day. Not the way I raised you to live."

Lisa exchanged a look with her mother. Both of them had heard this speech plenty of times before.

As different from her husband as night from day, Ellen Woodrow was short, softly rounded and quiet natured. Perfectly content to live in the shadows of her husband's very public lifestyle, she was a homemaker in the old-fashioned sense of the word. She had never worked outside the house, enjoyed baking and sewing and had loved being a room mother and PTA member during her only child's school years.

There was no doubt that she adored her husband, and her habitual deference to him was by choice rather than coercion. Even as she had rebelled against that future for herself, Lisa had known that her mother was happy.

The only time Lisa had ever seen her mom stand up

to her dad was to defend Lisa's decision to enter law school. She had raised her daughter to follow her dreams, she'd asserted firmly. If Lisa had been content to follow in her mother's domestic footsteps, that would have been fine, but if her ambitions lay elsewhere, then she had her mother's full support. Woody's sputtering refusals had somehow faded away after that, grudging acceptance in their wake, and Lisa would always be grateful for her mother's intervention.

Which didn't mean her dad would ever be completely happy about her decision.

"I still like my job, Dad. I just needed a little break. While I'm here, Wade and I want to spend some time together to, um, see if there's still a spark between us," she finished lamely.

"You can't do that here? You have to travel with him?"

"And when would I see him here?" she countered. "If I want to see him at all I'll have to go to Pennsylvania. Besides, I've never really been behind the scenes at a race. I'm sure I would find it fascinating."

"You'll be in his way. I don't want you interfering with his concentration. We've got a race to win. Jake needs all the points he can accumulate to stay solidly in The Chase."

So that was the real problem, she thought in resignation. Not that she might be hurt again if her imaginary relationship with Wade fell through for a second time. But that she might interfere with Wade's work during a season that had a good chance of ending with Woody's first NASCAR NEXTEL Cup championship trophy.

Woody was already chafing at the enforced confinement that was keeping him from micromanaging at the race-track; this was just another way for him to try to minimize any problems that might develop in his absence.

"I won't interfere. Wade's already assured me that he'll be able to focus on winning even if I'm there."

"It doesn't look right, you staying in his motor coach when you aren't even married. I've already given my suite to someone else and it would be rude of me to take it back now for you. If I were going, it would be different, since you could stay with me, but those damn doctors won't let me travel for another month. At least, that's what they think."

"And they're right," Ellen said with a flash of deter-mination. "You aren't traveling until your doctor clears you, even if I have to tie you to your chair."

Woody chuckled and reached out to pat his wife's hand. "Okay, honey, don't get your panties in a twist. I'm trying to be good."

He'd mellowed in the past few years, Lisa mused. There was a time when her father would have been very impatient with her mom's attempt to get him to take care of himself. But that was before she'd developed a heart condition that now required constant monitoring and made both Lisa and her father aware that in her quiet, unassuming way, Ellen served as the solid center of their family.

But then his faint smile faded and he frowned at Lisa again. "It doesn't look right."

She sighed. "Daddy. I'm twenty-eight years old. I've

been out on my own for quite a while now. And besides, Wade said he'd bunk with Jake while I'm there. We just want to spend some time together during my vacation. I won't distract him and I won't get in his way, okay?"

Ellen tapped her chin thoughtfully, looking from her daughter to her husband, but she kept her opinion to herself, to Lisa's relief.

Woody reached for his despised aluminum walker that stood next to his chair. "I've got to get to work. Got three conference calls and two meetings scheduled before two o'clock this afternoon and then a workout with the physical therapist. We'll talk about this later, Lisa."

"We can talk about it, but I'm still going," she replied, giving him a little smile to soften the remark.

Grumbling beneath his breath, Woody thumped out of the kitchen, leaving Lisa sitting alone with her mother.

"More coffee, honey?" Ellen asked.

Lisa shook her head. "Actually, I have a couple of calls to make myself this morning."

"Just like your daddy," Ellen murmured with an indulgent shake of her still-blond, stylist-enhanced hair. "Working even on vacation."

"Just a couple of things I'm trying to monitor long-distance while I'm away."

"Mmm. So the real reason you took this long vacation was to try to renew your relationship with Wade? You certainly kept that a secret."

Trying to stick to the cover story she and Wade had concocted—despite her guilt about doing so—Lisa sipped her coffee and shrugged, letting that serve as her answer.

Her mom looked worried. "I know you and Wade have never stopped loving each other. But I don't know how much either of you has changed since the last time you were together. I hope you'll be careful, Lisa. I would hate to see you hurt as badly as you were last time."

There were so many things in that little speech that Lisa wanted to address. Her mother didn't think she had changed after all this time, after finishing law school and embarking on a challenging career? She made it sound as if Wade had been the one to end the engagement rather than Lisa herself.

And what made her mom think that she and Wade still loved each other? They had barely spoken during the past six years. Obviously, they had both moved on.

Because none of those comments fit into the cover story intended to protect her parents from the unnerving truth, Lisa swallowed her questions and said simply, "I'll be careful, Mom. It's just a vacation, really. A chance to spend some time at the track, watch an entire race weekend. I've never really done much of that, you know."

"That's true," her mom acknowledged. "Your daddy always thought of racing as a 'man's' sport. He liked keeping that part of his life separate from his home life. He's getting better about that, though. As racing has opened up more to women, your father has come around. He has quite a few women on his payroll now—mostly in the offices, but a few in the shops. One's an engineer."

"That is quite progressive for Dad," Lisa said, trying to smile. As she moved the conversation along—and far away from potentially dangerous territory—she was still fretting over her mother's assertion that Wade was in love with her.

Ridiculous, of course, and completely misguided, but she couldn't seem to get the casually spoken words out of her mind.

CHAPTER THREE

WADE TOOK LISA TO DINNER THAT evening at an Italian restaurant that had once been their favorite. Ellen extended an invitation to them to dine at home, but Lisa declined, saying she and Wade needed some time together before leaving the next afternoon for Pennsylvania.

She'd been torn by that choice. As reluctant as she was to be alone with Wade for even one meal, she was also disinclined to spend time with him and her parents.

Despite their agreement to mislead her parents—at least for now—about the real purpose for her present alliance with Wade, she didn't want to have to spend an entire evening pretending to be falling for him again. She wasn't sure she was that good of an actor. It was much safer, all in all, for them to be alone where they could be completely frank about the pragmatic nature of their temporary partnership.

Apparently, she wasn't the only one who had misgivings about them spending too much time together. Jake Hinson joined them at the restaurant, obviously at Wade's invitation.

Wade and Lisa had just been seated when the hostess brought Jake to their table. Lisa hid her surprise as she greeted the good-looking driver, who was already the object of attention from other diners in the restaurant.

She had always thought there was something about the way a driver walked that singled him out even to people who didn't follow racing. A cocky assurance that served him well on the track, a no-nonsense gait that took him where he wanted to go swiftly and with few distractions. Accustomed to walking and signing autographs at the same time, he kept his eyes on the goal, but he was aware of everything that went on around him—another benefit of driving around a hundred and eighty miles an hour only inches away from the other forty-two equally fast cars on the track.

Or maybe she was just romanticizing the profession, she thought with a smothered smile. "Hello, Jake."

Dark haired and dark eyed, with a dimpled smile that had graced the cover of quite a few magazines, Jake searched her face as he slid into one of the two empty chairs at the table. "Hey, Lisa. How are you doing?"

Something about the concern in his voice gave her a clue that he and Wade had been talking. "Wade told you why I'm here?"

Both men nodded. "I figured Jake could help us out at the track," Wade explained. "I'll be bunking with him while you're in my coach and he can help me keep an eye out for you."

"I don't need either of you keeping an eye out for me," she said, shaking her head. "I don't expect any trouble, but if anything crops up, I can handle it."

"Oh, yeah? And how do you plan to do that?" Wade asked a bit too politely.

"I'm as capable as anyone of calling 9-1-1. I'll keep my cell phone with me at all times."

"Good plan," Jake said conciliatorily. "But it still doesn't hurt to have reinforcements on your side."

She deliberately soothed her frown. She wasn't going to spend the entire meal arguing with them, she promised herself. Instead, she changed the subject. "So, Jake, I hear your season is going very well so far."

Though she wouldn't admit it tonight, Lisa rarely missed watching a race. She spent almost every Sunday afternoon sprawled on her bed with a pile of paperwork, race coverage blaring from her TV. No matter how hard she always tried to resist, her eyes turned inexorably toward the screen whenever Wade was even mentioned.

He flashed a grin. "Nineteen races down and I'm fifth in points. All I've got to do is race clean and finish well for seven more events and I've got a shot at the Championship."

Though Woody's other three drivers were doing well this season, thirty-year-old Jake, competing in his third season of full-time NASCAR NEXTEL Cup racing, was considered the best bet to take it all. Wade and Jake made a formidable team, their close friendship seeming to give them the ability to communicate almost psychically at times.

Wade had been Jake's crew chief since Jake moved to NASCAR NEXTEL Cup racing from the NASCAR Busch Series, where he'd been extremely successful, taking the championship his final full-time year there. Though she hadn't been around much during those years, Lisa had heard from her mother that the two had bonded like long-lost brothers almost from the beginning. She figured their mutual obsession for the sport, combined with an overwhelming drive to win, was the real foundation for their friendship.

She had met Jake only a few times through her father, but she had always liked what she'd seen of him. He had a reputation for being congenial and even-tempered, a fierce competitor, but a clean racer. Not one of the young hotheads, or one of those few drivers with an air of arrogant entitlement, Jake seemed genuinely happy to be allowed to pursue a career he loved and grateful to his owner, his team, his sponsors and his fans for supporting him.

"I'm glad things are going so well for you," she said, looking directly at Jake as she spoke. "I know Dad's really pleased with the way the season's going."

Jake chuckled. "It's always good to keep the owner happy."

A server approached the table—a young man who obviously recognized Jake and Wade, and was rather star-struck waiting on them—and they placed their orders. When the server moved away, Lisa felt obligated to say something to fill the slightly awkward silence left behind.

"How do you like your chances this weekend?" she asked Jake. "I've never been to this race, so it will be a new experience for me."

Jake grimaced. "It's a tough track. It's got three straights, each one a different length, and three corners, all with different levels of banking. We go as fast there as at any superspeedway, but then we have to downshift into the curves, the way we would at a road course. Tough on the engines. There's always a few that give out toward the end of the race. And this is also where we face the toughest turn in racing." He exaggerated a shudder. "Turn Two. You go into that one single file, or you smack the wall."

"Yeah, but Turn Three is wide enough for some good racing," Wade interjected, also speaking for Lisa's benefit. "You can really build up some momentum there. Which is why we're setting the car up more for Turn Three than Turns One and Two."

"Making Turn Two even more difficult for the driver," Jake grumbled.

"You just let me know what you need and I'll give it to you," Wade promised him.

Jake made a comment about being too loose the last time he'd raced in Pennsylvania, and Wade assured him that the problem had been addressed for the upcoming event. They fell into a discussion about track bars and spring rubbers and wedge adjustments and Lisa zoned out, entertaining herself by dipping bread into herbed oil.

She'd heard dozens of talks like this, of course, back when she and Wade had dated, when he was still moving up through the ranks toward crew chief. Her father's star driver then had been Ed Jablonski, a solid racer who finished several times in the top five in points, twice in second place. Jake had been moved up the year after Ed retired due to health problems.

Jake and Wade had won their third NASCAR NEXTEL Cup race together, finishing near the top enough times that season for Jake to be named rookie of the year. Ever since, it had been taken almost for granted in the sport that Jake would eventually win a championship, a prediction bolstered by seven more wins, two of them earlier this season. He'd barely made The Chase last season, but a run of bad luck at the final racetracks had kept him in fourth place rather than first, at the end of the season.

"We're being rude," Jake said, brought back to his surroundings when their food was delivered to the table. "Sitting here talking about mechanical stuff when we have a beautiful civilian at the table with us."

Even as she told herself it was just a line, Lisa still found herself charmed by Jake's smile. Those dimples should be registered as lethal weapons, she thought. "Don't mind me. I'm used to this."

"Which doesn't make it any more polite," he insisted. "Tell me about your job in Chicago. Is being a prosecutor as exciting as it looks on TV?"

"Hardly. Trust me, my present circumstances are extremely unusual. If my boss hadn't been the overcautious type, I never would have been put on leave just because of one thug's threats."

"More than threats, apparently," Wade murmured, cutting into his manicotti. "You said people have already been injured and someone tried to break into your home. I think your boss had good reason to be cautious."

She shrugged. "Maybe."

Jake took a sip of his wine and set his glass on the table. "You were right to come to Wade for help. We'll keep you safe at the track."

Frowning, Lisa clarified, "I didn't exactly come to Wade. He sort of found out about my situation accidentally and he offered to help. I accepted because I don't want to upset my parents."

"Good plan. Your folks have enough to worry about now, what with your dad's recuperation and all."

"That's what I thought."

"So it's a good thing you and Wade stayed friendly, huh? You don't see many exes who can turn to each other in a time of crisis like this."

Lisa met Wade's gaze across the table, then forced a smile. "Wade has been very generous to offer his help."

"I told Lisa I'd keep out of her way," Wade added with a slight shrug. "We stay too busy at the track for her to have to worry about spending too much time with me."

Something about the way he said that piqued her pride. "I'm not worried about spending time with you. I'm perfectly comfortable being around you."

"Yeah," Wade muttered. "Me, too."

Jake looked from one of them to the other. "So y'all were really engaged, huh?"

"We were very young then," Lisa said, stabbing a bit too forcefully into her food.

"Naive," Wade added.

She flicked him a glance. "Impressionable."

"Gullible."

Jake's mouth twitched with a smile. "I see. I'm glad you both got over it."

"Completely," Lisa assured him.

"Absolutely," Wade seconded.

"Okay. So, Lisa, tell me more stories about prosecuting in the big city."

Because it was much easier to talk about her job than her long-ago engagement, she shared a few anecdotes about some of her more interesting cases while they finished their meal. Jake asked a lot of questions and seemed very interested in her answers, though she didn't know if he really was or if he was simply being polite.

Wade said little, but she knew he listened to every word she said. Maybe he was thinking about how different things would be—for both of them—if she had never left.

She couldn't say she'd never thought along those lines, herself, on occasion. But she could say she had made the right decision, no matter how painful it had been.

THE PENNSYLVANIA RACETRACK was arguably located in the most romantic of all the NASCAR venues. Famed as a honeymoon setting, the Pocono Mountains provided breathtaking scenery and plenty of intimate destinations. None of which had anything to do with her and Wade, of course, Lisa assured herself as they drove through the tunnel beneath the infamous Turn Two and onto the infield of the track.

Back when she and Wade had been an item, he had stayed in motel rooms during the racing season. Now he spent race weekends in his own luxury motor home parked in the infield of the track. He told her that owning a motor home had become quite common for drivers and owners, but most of the crew chiefs still stayed in nearby motels, as did most of the other racing employees who were only in town for a weekend and were then off to the next venue.

To save time, a driver who worked solely for Wade moved the motor home from one track to the next, allowing Wade to fly into the area on Thursday and have his home-away-from-home waiting for him, fully stocked and ready for him to occupy. He said it gave him a sanctuary during the few free minutes he could grab and the comfort of having his own things around him, set up exactly the way he liked them.

Lisa knew Jake and the other drivers on her father's team also had their own custom motor coaches, though as far as she was aware none of the other crew chiefs had found it worthwhile to make that significant financial investment. Her dad preferred hotel suites for himself, away from the noise and bustle of the track crowds. He reserved his regular suites a year in advance, with car and driver ready at a moment's notice to take him to the tracks.

Having never seen Wade's motor home, she was rather startled when he escorted her inside Thursday afternoon. Some forty-feet long, with hydraulically operated sliders on both sides that pushed out to almost double the living space, the coach was as comfortable and as beautifully decorated as any full-time apartment. Much nicer than the little one-bedroom place he had rented back when they'd dated, while he was still working his way up through the Woodrow Racing organization.

Like the sleek, racy outside, the color scheme inside was also gray and deep purple. It matched Jake's Number 82 car, which was painted in a splashy purple and silver combination, embellished with the swirling logo of his primary sponsor, Vaughan Tools. That same purple was visible here, in upholstery and draperies, accented by grays ranging from pearl to charcoal. Chrome and neon, large-screen plasma TVs and built-in stereo systems, top of the line appliances and deep, indulgent cushions. Not exactly subtle and hardly what she would have predicted from Wade.

"Interesting," she murmured, looking around. "Not what I expected."

Wade's smile was crooked, a little sheepish. "There were all these choices to make—gave me a headache. I finally asked the saleswoman to handle the details for me."

"She chose the best of everything, apparently."

He shrugged. "Well, she did go all out. I gave her a price limit and she took it from there. Considering that I spend at least thirty-six weekends a year in this bus, it was well worth the investment. Since I'm single and not home much, I've kept my house in North Carolina pretty modest, not like the mansions most of the owners and drivers maintain, so this feels more like my real home sometimes."

She lifted an eyebrow. "You certainly don't have to justify your indulgences to me."

"I'm not." And then he made a face. "Well, maybe I am, a little. I mean, you're used to this kind of lifestyle, considering your background, but my roots are strictly blue-collar. It still sort of blows my mind that I can afford things like this now, as long as I keep a pretty close eye on my budget."

She couldn't help laughing. "If you could see my apartment in Chicago, you'd realize that I know all about living within a budget. Prosecutors hardly get rich, you know. I live on my own salary, not on my father's money. This place looks downright luxurious to me."

What might have been a glimmer of respect flickered through his brown eyes. "Make yourself at home here. Consider yourself on vacation."

She looked around at the comfortable surroundings again. "I guess I haven't stopped to think about exactly how much I'm putting you out this weekend. I'm sorry, Wade, I should have gone somewhere else. You need to concentrate and you deserve to stay in your own—"

"Lees," he interrupted firmly, stopping her mid-word. "I wouldn't have suggested it if I minded. After hearing about your ordeal, there's no way I could have concentrated on the race without knowing for sure that you were safe. I'll be fine bunking with Jake. It's a way of keeping him out of trouble this weekend."

"You should at least get to sleep on your own bed. I could always take the couch. I bet it folds out into a bed."

"It does." But then he shook his head. "I'll stay with Jake. All in all, I think that's best."

Because it didn't look right for them to share a motor home, as her father had said? Or was there another reason he didn't want to be in such close quarters with her this weekend?

Deciding she'd better not think about that right now, she moistened her suddenly dry lips. "You're being very generous, Wade. Thank you."

His expression was suddenly closed to her. "I'd do the same for any of my friends."

He considered her a friend? Interesting. She couldn't say her feelings for him were quite so simple.

He took a step backward from her. "Your bags have been placed in the bedroom. I had a couple of drawers emptied out for you, so feel free to unpack. Let me show you a few things here in the coach and then I should head over to the garage. If you need to reach me for any reason, you can call me on my cell."

She followed dutifully while he demonstrated touch-pad remote controls and pop-up plasma TV screens, showed her hidden panels in the galley and bathroom and the electric shades on every window. She'd never been in one of these things, since her father disliked them. She was amazed by how many amenities had been incorporated. There was even a ceiling fan in the bedroom, built into a lighted ceiling recess.

Wade was right, of course, she thought after he left her. She had grown up with money and luxuries. Though she had been honest about living on her salary for the past few years, staying on a budget and counting her pennies at times, she had always had the security of knowing she had the trust fund her father had set up for her to fall back on if necessary.

Wade's background was much less privileged. He had told her his family had been a dysfunctional one. His flighty and unreliable parents had pretty much neglected their two sons, who'd both struck out on their own as soon as they were legally of age. Lisa's home life might not have been exactly what she would have chosen, with her workaholic father and happy homemaker mother, but at least she had never doubted that her parents loved her. Well, with her father, almost never. Wade hadn't been blessed with that comfort.

He didn't see his parents much now, or at least, not the last she'd heard, nor was he close to his brother. His life was racing, not family—a realization that she should have come to much sooner than she actually had. She blamed her youth and foolishly romantic daydreams for keeping her blind to the facts for so long.

She would have to be very careful over the next few days not to fool herself into thinking that anything had changed.

EVEN THOUGH WADE'S motor home in this restricted parking lot was surrounded by those of other drivers and owners—some of their families she could hear socializing outside despite the impressive sound-proofing—Lisa stayed inside Thursday. She spent the afternoon catching up on a stack of paperwork she'd brought with her, setting up her laptop computer and handling her e-mail that had piled up.

She might be on a leave of absence, but work was never far away from her mind. The irony of that didn't escape her. It had been Wade's obsession with his job that had broken them up, but now she was as much of a workaholic as he'd ever been.

It was equally ironic that she was now trapped in what amounted to his home while he concentrated on his duties, probably having forgotten that she was even here. This was exactly what she had been afraid of when she'd left him, she thought with a wry shake of her head. And this time, she'd deliberately put herself here. But at least she had work of her own to concentrate on.

She pulled her computer in front of her again, grateful that she had something more important to do than to cook Wade's dinner and wait impatiently for him to appear in the doorway.

As it happened, she was so deeply immersed in work that she didn't even hear him when he tapped on the door early that evening. It took a buzz from the intercom system to rouse her. As he had instructed, she checked the monitor before she opened the door.

He nodded his approval of her caution. "Were you asleep?"

"No. I was working. How were things in the garage?"

"Looking good so far. Everything arrived in one piece."

"That's always good."

Chit-chat out of the way, Wade got to the point. "Some of us are going out to dinner. Want to come?"

She almost declined. She knew the motor home had been stocked with food and she could easily prepare a quick meal for herself. But then she figured she might as well go. After all, this was her chance to get an inside look at the world of racing that so consumed her father and former fiancé.

"Sure," she said, moving out of the doorway. "Do I have time to freshen up first?"

Following her into the living area, he glanced curiously at the laptop and files stacked on the small built-in dining table and nodded. "We've got about twenty minutes before we're supposed to meet Jake and the others."

"That's more than enough time," she assured him, heading for the bedroom. "I'll be right back."

IN ADDITION TO LISA, Wade and Jake, the diners included another Woodrow Racing driver, Ronnie Short, and his wife, Katie, and Ronnie's crew chief, Joe "Digger" Barkley. It was a genial, casual crowd and Lisa could tell immediately that they were all friends as well as teammates. She also knew that friendship didn't keep them from being fierce competitors on the racetrack.

Lisa had met everyone at some point during the past few years, except for Katie Short, who she met for the first time tonight. A pudgy, pleasant-faced redhead, Katie was the type whose smile could light up a room and whose laughter could only be described as infectious. Lisa liked her immediately.

The restaurant specialized in steak and ribs, and this group was populated by carnivores who took advantage of the menu, Lisa noted wryly. She ordered grilled chicken with grilled vegetables on the side.

Talk around the table centered on work, of course, with the men focusing on qualifying the next day. From what Lisa understood, Wade was worried about engine failures for the upcoming race, while Digger seemed more concerned about wrecks on Turn Two. She'd figured out that crew chiefs were always worried about something; they were paid well to worry—which probably explained why neither of the drivers looked overly perturbed.

Ronnie talked about the other drivers, especially one rookie who'd been causing him problems during the season. "I swear, the guy's a menace on the track," he growled, his deeply tanned face creased with a scowl. "He never should have been moved up. He gets in my way Sunday, he and I are going to be having a little talk afterward."

His wife shook her head, then turned to Lisa. "Men," she muttered. "I swear, they just aren't much different at this age than the five year olds I teach in kindergarten."

Lisa chuckled. "You are pretty much surrounded by testosterone on a daily basis," she said, keeping her voice low so their conversation remained between the girls. "How do you stay sane?"

"Who says I do?" Katie retorted. "After two years of marriage to a racer, I'm starting to get a little peculiar myself."

Apparently, the men had been paying more attention than Lisa thought.

"See what you missed, Lisa?" Digger asked with his

usual lack of tact. "If you'd married Ice here, like you were going to, you'd be as crazy as the rest of us by now. Now here you are back to try it again."

CHAPTER FOUR

AN AWKWARD SILENCE FOLLOWED Digger's heavy-handed jest. Lisa noted the sharp look Wade shot at his business associate. He was obviously as embarrassed as she was by the joking reference to their former relationship.

"You and Wade were engaged?" Katie blurted in surprise. "I'd heard you once dated but I didn't know you were engaged."

"It was a long time ago," Lisa explained, trying to keep her expression pleasant and unruffled. She was actually surprised that Katie hadn't heard that tidbit through the gossip that seemed to spread like wildfire through any group of associates. "We were very young."

"Lisa realized she had dreams of her own she wanted to pursue," Wade added.

Lisa felt her left eyebrow rise a fraction of an inch. Wade sounded as if he understood better than she realized why she'd felt the need to leave. He didn't seem to be just parroting the excuse she had used.

She had often wondered if he was as relieved as she was that they hadn't gone through with the wedding. Was he really being as supportive as he sounded or was he just glad she'd found a way out that had saved face for both of them?

"So now you're dating each other again?" Ronnie asked, looking confused.

Lisa and Wade exchanged a quick look, then Wade said, "We're still friends. Lisa's been so busy with her career that she hasn't had much chance to hang around the track over the past few years. She's on a well-deserved vacation now, so I offered to let her hang with me behind the scenes, so to speak."

"My father never encouraged me to visit the tracks," Lisa added. "He liked keeping his home life completely separate from the racing world."

"Some men are like that," Katie said with a nod. "Either they want their families around every minute, or not at all."

"Most of the drivers who don't want them around have a reason," Digger muttered. "They don't want to get caught chasing the women—not that your daddy ever did that," he added quickly to Lisa. "Everyone knows Woody ain't one for fooling around. Racing, that's his passion."

While Wade, Jake and Ronnie rolled their eyes in response to Digger's usual lack of tact, Lisa only smiled. She had never suspected her father of being unfaithful to her mother. Partly because he loved the wife he kept sheltered and pampered at home, but also because of what Digger had said. Her dad's passion was channeled into business, not romance. Given a choice between a buxom beauty queen and a shiny new trophy to display in his lavish office, Woody wouldn't give the lady a second glance.

Lisa had always thought Wade would make the same sort of husband. Faithful, but constantly distracted, nevertheless. Any woman who eventually landed him would have to have a very satisfying life of her own to keep from feeling ignored and neglected. But why was she letting herself think about that again now?

Katie made a joking comment about traveling close to Ronnie to keep him on the straight and narrow when it came to the women who hung around the tracks. Ronnie assured her that he was much too frightened of her temper to take any foolish risks. Especially, he added with a proud grin, since pregnant women were known to be particularly vicious.

Lisa hadn't been aware that Katie was pregnant, which led to a new discussion about the baby that was due in just over five months. It was obvious that both soon-to-be parents were thrilled and impatient. Wade and Jake seemed bemused by the whole thing.

Digger, twice divorced and with three nearly grown offspring of his own, was the old hand with plenty of advice to dispense about child raising—which he proceeded to do right then. Ronnie laughed and reminded Digger that his job was to supervise Ronnie's racing, not his parenting.

Relieved that the conversation had moved away from her history with Wade, Lisa quietly finished her dinner.

They were almost finished with dessert when a young boy, perhaps twelve, approached the table with an expression that combined excitement and anxiety. He held a white paper napkin and a pen in his hand, and he looked prepared to run at a moment's notice. "Excuse me, Mr. Hinson?" he said to Jake in a voice that quivered just a little.

No one at the table seemed surprised by the interruption. Jake smiled warmly at the boy. "What can I do for you?"

The boy held out the napkin. "Would you mind signing an autograph? And you, too, Mr. Short. I like watching you race, too."

Both Jake and Ronnie agreed to sign the napkin. Encouraged by his success, the boy demonstrated his knowledge of the sport by identifying Wade and Digger by name and asking the crew chiefs to sign next to their drivers' autographs. He looked thrilled when they obliged.

"We'd better leave now," Wade murmured, motioning for their server. "Once it gets started, it's hard to get away."

Sure enough, another few autograph-seekers hurried to the table after the boy's approach. A couple of young women in tops that just barely covered their attributes vied for Jake's attention, but he showed them no more interest than he had the others, to their obvious disappointment. One of them batted her lashes at Ronnie a couple of times, but a firmly cleared throat and a warning frown from Katie sent them on their way with their autographs clutched in manicured hands.

Accustomed to racing celebrity clientele, the restaurant management put an end to the impromptu session then, escorting them out in a way that politely discouraged any further requests.

Saying good-night to the others, Lisa, Wade and Jake climbed into the car Wade had rented for the evening. With Wade behind the wheel and Lisa in the backseat, they headed toward the racetrack. She realized that she was more tired than she might have expected. She only hoped she would be able to sleep in a strange bed—Wade's bed.

"LET ME GET THIS STRAIGHT. You're at the racetrack on the day of qualifying, you have access to the garage where all the hot drivers hang out and you're sitting in a motor home working?"

"When you say it like that you almost make me sound dull," Lisa teased her friend and coworker, Davida White, at just after noon on Friday. Bored and a bit lonely sitting in Wade's motor home all morning, she'd called her office for an update and Davida had answered.

"One would think," Davida retorted. "Get out there, girl, and flirt with some of those hotties. And if you happen to bring me back a few autographed glossies, I won't complain."

"The hotties are all too busy trying to get into the race to flirt this afternoon. But I could probably score you a few autographs before I leave, if you want," she added, remembering how willingly Jake and Ronnie had signed the night before after dinner. "Anyone in particular?"

Davida breathlessly named one of the most popular young drivers in the sport, adding that she wouldn't mind having Jake Hinson's photo, either.

Lisa guaranteed the latter and promised to try for the former, making a mental note to ask Wade if he could help her out on that one. Davida was a good friend, and probably the biggest NASCAR fan Lisa knew back in Chicago. She was also the only one who made the connection between Lisa, NASCAR and her well-known father. Davida had kept that confidence to herself. This was the least she could do in return.

"I'd really like to get back to work," she said. "How's the search for Norris coming?"

"Not good," Davida replied, her tone growing serious. "Someone took a drive-by shot at Joe Engler last night. Whoever it was got away, but everyone's pretty sure it was either Norris or one of his buddies."

Lisa was horrified to hear the news about her co-prosecutor, who had refused to take a leave of absence from work despite the threats against him. "Someone shot Joe? Is he all right?"

"He's in the hospital. He's going to be okay, but he was hurt pretty bad. You'd better stay where you are, Lisa."

Lisa moistened her lips. "Yeah. I guess I will."

Maybe she was a coward, but she had thought Joe was being reckless by staying on the job and in public view even after receiving several threats from Norris. Now she'd been shown to be right. She wished she'd been wrong.

The pleasure robbed from their conversation now, Lisa and Davida spoke for only a few more minutes before Lisa hung up. She sat at the table behind her computer for several long minutes, staring blankly at the screen.

Someone tapped on the door, making her jump about six inches. She took a deep breath to steady herself and checked the monitor before opening the door. "What's up?"

"I had a few free minutes," Wade said with a shrug. "I thought I'd say hi. See if you needed anything."

She didn't remember him ever taking even a few minutes away from work on qualifying day. "Thanks, but I'm fine. Don't let me keep you away from your responsibilities."

His gaze was too shrewd on her face. "What's wrong? You look like something's bothering you."

She hesitated, then decided she might as well answer honestly. "One of my coworkers was injured in a drive-by shooting. They're pretty sure Jesse Norris was behind it."

Wade's expression went grim. "Why can't they catch that guy? You're the one who pointed out that it isn't as if he's lying low."

"No, but he's had years of experience at evading the law. And he has help."

"Is there any chance he knows where you are?"

"I don't suppose it would be too hard to find out. But the odds of him following me here—and then getting to me if he did—are really slim, Wade. He's probably satisfied that he scared me into running."

Wade must have heard chagrin in her voice. "You did the right thing, Lees. You couldn't have stayed there."

"I know," she conceded. "But I hate that he's controlling my life right now."

"He's not. You made the choice to go home—and you

made the choice to join me here," he reminded her. "You're in control here and you have to let the authorities be in charge back there."

She nodded unhappily.

"Look, why don't you come with me for a while? You can watch Jake qualify from the top of the hauler. The car's handling good today. We're expecting a great run."

"I don't want to get in your way."

"So don't get in my way," he said with a shrug. "Doesn't mean you can't watch the action."

She looked at the computer and paperwork sitting on the table, and then at Wade, who was waiting impatiently for her reply. "Okay," she said. "I'd like to watch. Thanks."

He nodded. "Grab your ID and let's go."

She donned the lanyard that held a plastic case displaying her garage pass. Officially authorized, she stepped outside with Wade.

JAKE TOOK THE POLE. Ronnie qualified fifth, the third Woodrow Racing driver, Mike Overstreet, in the eleventh position, and the youngest driver on the team, rookie Scott Rivers, also in the top twenty.

There was great satisfaction in the garage area that the cars had performed so well, but no one was more pleased than Jake. Wade could see the joy in his driver's eyes, the anticipation of a championship that would validate his many years of hard work and sacrifice.

He felt that anticipation, himself, of course. A crew chief shared in the glory when his driver won a championship. The entire team celebrated that victory, which wouldn't be possible without all of them working together. If anyone had asked Wade any time over the past half of his life what would make him the happiest, he would have said it was being the crew chief on a championship team. And now that goal was in sight.

True, there were still a few races to go until the final ten and the championship. Wade had learned long ago that there was no such thing as a guarantee when it came to racing. But Jake was sitting pretty in points and the crew was working like a well-oiled machine. Wade was as close to confident as he could be that this season would be the one.

So why wasn't he feeling more of the same jubilation the rest of the team displayed as they gathered in Victory Lane for the pole winner's photo session? Rather than concentrating on the celebration—which would be short-lived, since they would be turning their attentions almost immediately to tomorrow's practice session—he found himself constantly looking for Lisa. Reassuring himself that she was safe.

So much for his promise to himself that she wouldn't interfere with his concentration this weekend.

He noticed that she had been taken under Katie Short's wing for the afternoon. They looked as though they were getting pretty cozy and he wasn't sure how he felt about that. Were they talking about him?

They made an interesting pair, the tall, thin, blond attorney and the short, chubby red-haired kindergarten teacher. Just looking at Lisa still made his heart skip a beat, something it had never done for anyone else. The thought of anything happening to her…well, it made it damned hard for him to smile for the photographers.

"What's the problem, Ice?"

Wade glanced at Jake, who ran a hand through his helmet-tousled dark hair as he gave his crew chief a curious once-over. Not that his messy hair seemed to bother any of the women hanging around the perimeters of Victory Lane wearing Jake Hinson T-shirts and hoping to catch his eye.

"I'm sorry, what did you say?"

Jake's eyebrows rose in response to Wade's uncharacteristic distraction. "I asked what's wrong. Dude, I got the pole. How come you're not grinning?"

In a low voice that couldn't carry over the crowd noise surrounding them, Wade gave Jake a succinct summary of what Lisa had told him earlier.

Looking toward Lisa, Jake frowned. "Damn. No wonder you look worried. Think we should beef up security around her?"

"Smile," Wade ordered him quickly. "And look away from Lisa. The media hasn't actually connected her to what's happened in Chicago yet, and she doesn't want them to. So far the Chicago story hasn't hit the national media. It's just a local mess involving a thug with a vendetta against a low-profile prosecution team. If anyone were to figure out that one of those young prosecutors is Woody's daughter, they'd blow it all out of proportion and Lisa's folks would get upset."

Though Jake cooperated with instructions to smile and wave to his fans, he murmured, "She should probably consider telling them. This sort of thing tends to get out. You know what we say. There are no secrets in the racing world."

"She'll tell them—in her own time."

Jake turned and clapped Wade on the shoulder, as though still celebrating their accomplishment that afternoon. "So all we have to do is keep her alive until she gets the chance to talk to them."

Wade knew it was meant as a joke—admittedly a dark one. He didn't find it at all funny. The face Jake made after hearing his own poor jest indicated that he had spoken without thinking and already regretted the words.

"Hey, Jake. Ice. Look over here, guys."

They turned simultaneously, automatically smiling for the camera. Wade only hoped the lens didn't pick up the worry he suspected was reflected in his eyes.

KATIE INVITED LISA BACK to her motor home for tea after the qualifying and Lisa accepted. Just in case he would be worried if she disappeared without explanation, she sent a message to Wade where she would be.

Katie chattered nonstop from the time they left the uniquely stable-styled white garages until they walked into her motor home, which, for some odd reason, Katie referred to as "Clyde."

"Clyde?" Lisa repeated, glancing around the luxurious celery, butter and cream colored Prevost that made Wade's motor home look almost modest in comparison.

"Well, we have to call it something," Katie said, as if it made perfect sense. "You know, like, I'm going back to Clyde now. And, if you need me, I'll be with Clyde. You know."

Lisa laughed. "Okay. Hi, Clyde. Nice to meet you."

Giggling, Katie filled the teapot. "I know, it's sort of silly. But when you spend as many weekends on the road as we do, you come up with all sorts of odd ways to entertain yourself."

At Katie's gestured invitation, Lisa sank onto the soft, cream-colored leather sofa that dominated the salon part of the motor home. "So this is what you do during your time off? Travel with Ronnie?"

She hadn't meant for the question to sound critical, but she grimaced as she heard her own words. "I didn't mean—"

"I know what you meant," Katie said matter-of-factly, handing her a cup and saucer. "I still have a life of my own. I'm a teacher—and a good one. I'll probably go back to it someday. But for now, I want to concentrate on Ronnie and the baby."

"How did you meet Ronnie?"

Katie smiled. "He was signing autographs at a car dealership in my hometown. I took my nephews to see him. One of my nephews got so excited that he spilled a snow cone all over poor Ronnie. I got flustered and I started apologizing and trying to wipe him off with my hands—and well…he liked it."

Thinking of the way Ronnie looked at his sweet-faced wife, Lisa had no doubt that he'd fallen hard and fast for her. "I'm sure he did."

"He asked me out right then. I almost said no. I mean,

the guy was signing autographs, for Pete's sake. No one ever asks a kindergarten teacher for an autograph, unless it's at the bottom of a student progress report. But then he smiled at me—and I heard myself saying yes. Eight months later, we were married. Now we're starting a family and I couldn't be happier."

She took a sip of her tea, then continued reflectively, "I'm not saying it's the easiest thing in the world, being married to a driver. The traveling gets old, but so does staying at home while he's away for more than half the year. And although the cars are getting safer every season, I still worry every time he gets involved in a crash on the track. He works six days out of most weeks during the season, sometimes from dawn until long after dark. The money's good, of course, but sometimes it feels as if we don't have time to enjoy it."

Lisa remembered how rarely she saw her own workaholic father when she was growing up. "Are you going to continue to travel with Ronnie after the baby's born?"

"Oh, sure. Maybe not quite as much as I do now, but as often as possible. The NASCAR family programs are wonderful and the kids make so many good friends during all the activities that are arranged for them. I want Ronnie to know his kids and vice versa."

Lisa couldn't help thinking again of her own childhood and how much she would have enjoyed traveling with her father and getting to know other children whose parents were obsessed with racing.

"Besides," Katie added impishly, "I like to remind everyone that my Ronnie is very much taken. I know he's not considered one of the heartthrob racers, but I make it very clear that he's all mine."

"I think Ronnie is as much a heartthrob as anyone," Lisa replied immediately. "And I don't think you have to worry about the women. Ronnie doesn't see anyone but you."

"That's what I keep telling him. You want a cookie or something? I'm always hungry after qualifying. Oh, who am I kidding? Since I got pregnant, I'm just always hungry. Period."

Though she wasn't particularly hungry, Lisa accepted a cookie from her hostess. She hadn't had much appetite since she'd been forced to leave Chicago, and today's news hadn't done much to change that situation. Still, the homemade oatmeal-raisin cookie was very good and before she knew it, she was eating another one while listening to Katie rattle cheerfully about everything beneath the racing sun.

It was truly impressive how quickly Katie could move from one topic to another. She flitted from fairly innocuous gossip about other people on the circuit, to hints for cooking on the road, to Ronnie's chances of making The Chase, to asking questions about Lisa's job as a prosecutor—almost without pausing between topics.

Gamely following the changes, Lisa talked a little about her job. She had no intention originally to talk about the circumstances that had landed her in her ex-fiancé's motor home, but somehow the words just started tumbling from her. Maybe she was still in shock after hearing about Joe, or maybe it was just that Katie was such a receptive, sympathetic audience, but she had soon told the entire story to her new friend.

"Oh, my gosh," Katie exclaimed, her eyes wide. "I never knew your job was so dangerous."

"It isn't—not usually, anyway. I mean, defendants often make blustering threats against the prosecutors, the judges, even the juries, but there's rarely any follow-up. This guy, Norris, is just meaner, crazier and more determined than most—and he has friends who, for whatever their reasons, will do anything he asks of them."

"I don't blame you one bit for getting out of there. I'd be scared to death."

Lisa sighed. "I told myself I didn't want to run, but I have to admit it wasn't that hard for my boss to talk me into taking a leave of absence. I thought I'd just stay with my folks for a few weeks, but then I worried about upsetting them, if not actually putting them at some risk by being there."

"Wow. I hadn't even thought of that."

"I didn't, either, at first. But then I got spooked one night and…" She shrugged. "It was Wade's suggestion for me to stay in his motor home. I was hesitant at first, considering our history and not wanting to inconvenience him that much, but he can be persuasive when he tries."

Katie's expression turned speculative. "Wade's pretty private when it comes to his motor home. I don't think I've ever seen him even invite anyone inside, other than Jake and Ronnie and your dad. He must still care for you quite a lot if he was willing to actually let you live there for a few days."

CHAPTER FIVE

LISA COULDN'T REMEMBER the last time she had actually blushed. Probably since about the time she'd been hopelessly infatuated with Wade. Yet she felt her cheeks warm a bit in response to Katie's words, and she could only assume it was old habit that brought the color to her face. "He offered as much for my parents' sake as for mine. He's very fond of them."

"Maybe he's still fond of you, as well? I mean, I've always wondered why a guy as good-looking and interesting as Wade didn't have someone special in his life. Ronnie said it was because Wade's too married to his job to make time for anyone else, but I had a feeling there was more to it than that. I didn't know then, of course, that you two were engaged."

"It was a long time ago. We were just kids—well, I was. Wade's a few years older."

"So I take it you had a cordial parting of the ways? I ended an engagement once, and let me tell you, my ex-boyfriend wouldn't offer to help me with anything. He'd be more likely to offer to help the bad guy track me down. Let's just say the breakup did not go well."

Lisa sipped her tea to stall for a moment before answering. She thought back to the conversation she'd had with Wade the night she'd told him that she had been accepted into law school and that the wedding was off. She had braced herself for days, not certain what to expect from him. Would he yell at her? Argue with her in an attempt to change her mind? Would he drop to his knees and beg her to stay, telling her that she meant more to him than anything, including his job and that he couldn't live without her?

If she had secretly hoped for the latter, she was bound to be disappointed. Wade had listened to her carefully rehearsed speech with little expression on his face, saying not a word until she was finished. And then he had simply nodded, told her to call him if she ever needed anything from him and turned and walked out of the room without a backward glance.

The next time she'd seen him, he had treated her with the same polite distance that he'd displayed ever since. If she had broken his heart, or even bruised it a little, he hid it extremely well.

"Our breakup was amicable," she said, lowering her teacup. "It was my decision, but Wade took it well."

"Bummer. That had to hurt."

Her mouth twitching with an unexpected smile, Lisa nodded. "As a matter of fact, it did. It would have been much more flattering if he'd at least tried to talk me out of it."

"They don't call him 'Ice' for nothing."

"No. He totally earned that nickname." But he could

be warm, Lisa thought wistfully. Even passionate. He just rarely let anyone see that side of himself.

She had long believed his painful childhood was the reason he hid his feelings so well as an adult. He'd once told her that showing emotion had been a sign of weakness in his dysfunctional family. Showing any sort of vulnerability had been a bad idea, he'd added. She believed he had compared it specifically to bleeding in shark-infested waters.

"He seems like a nice man. I've always liked him, though I never felt as though I knew him very well."

"He is a good man. And very hard to get to know." Though there had been a time when she had known him probably better than anyone else. Or thought she had.

"You're getting along very well now. He seems awfully…well, aware of you. You know?"

"If you're trying to ask if Wade and I are getting back together, the answer is no. It didn't work the first time and I can't see it working between us now. But I am grateful to him for helping me out this week. I'd like to think we can always be friends."

It sounded so prim. So trite. And something told her that her new friend deserved better. "I could never compete with Wade's job. And I didn't want to spend the rest of my life trying. I haven't changed my mind about that."

"Oh." Katie looked vaguely disappointed. "But if he changed?"

"Then he wouldn't be Wade," Lisa said with a wry shrug.

Katie nodded as if Lisa's words made perfect sense. "Ronnie's as obsessed with racing as anyone. The morning of qualifying, the night before a race, it's as if he's with me physically, but his mind's already in the car. He's been known to eat an entire meal and then not remember a half hour later what I made for him."

"And that doesn't bother you?"

"Are you kidding? It drives me crazy. But I knew that about him when I married him. And I accepted it was part of the cost of being with him. It helps to know that he loves me at least as much as he does racing. And the times when I have his full attention are well worth the price.

"Besides," she added, "it isn't as if I'm moping around in limbo until he has time to pay attention to me. I've been doing some tutoring for kids in the family outreach program. And some of the other NASCAR wives and I like to play Bunko on Saturday nights while our husbands are busy. In a few months, I'll have the baby to keep me even busier. I've managed to find quite a bit of personal fulfillment being Ronnie's wife."

"I didn't mean to imply that you wouldn't. I just don't think it would be the same for me. Being a driver's wife, I mean. Or a crew chief's," Lisa added awkwardly.

And then she groaned and rolled her eyes. "Not that there's any chance of that. Wade and I both moved on a long time ago."

"Oh? So you have a boyfriend back in Chicago?"

"Well, no. I've been pretty busy with work."

"And Wade hardly ever sees anyone—too busy with

work, I guess." Katie's expression was just a bit too studiedly innocent.

"We've moved on," Lisa insisted.

"Of course you have. Do you want another cookie?"

Not at all certain she had convinced Katie that there was nothing new developing between her and Wade, Lisa politely declined the cookie and said she should probably get back to the motor home. She had a couple more calls to make that afternoon, she explained.

Katie didn't try to detain her any longer, but she made it clear that she was available whenever Lisa wanted companionship. Feeling as though she'd made a new friend, Lisa walked back alone to the motor home, aware of the curious looks from people she passed, most of whom had never seen her before.

She could hear a great deal of noise coming from another part of the infield, where the tailgating was in full swing among the fans who had parked their own motor homes and camper trailers there. She could smell the enticing aromas of barbecues and smoker-grills wafting through the hot summer air, and she predicted that the beer-fueled parties would continue well into the night.

It sounded like fun, she thought a bit wistfully as she keyed the security code into Wade's motor home. But she had to keep in mind that she didn't really belong here. This was Wade's world—and her father's and Katie's and all the other thousands of NASCAR participants and fans surrounding her on every side. Her place was back in Chicago—as soon as it was safe for her to return there.

Lisa had only been back in the motor home for maybe twenty minutes when Wade came to the door. "Want to go get something to eat?" he asked.

She'd planned to make use of the well-stocked kitchen, but she would always choose to have someone else cook for her when given the option. Besides, it got kind of lonely sitting in the motor home by herself. "Sure. I'd like that."

He nodded. "Are you ready?"

Having changed out of his splashy purple-and-silver sponsor colors, Wade now wore a white polo shirt embroidered on the pocket with the Woodrow Racing logo, navy chinos and black walking shoes. Deciding her bright yellow camp shirt worn over a matching tank top and dark jeans fit with his outfit, she nodded. "Let's go."

She expected to meet a group of his coworkers at the restaurant, as they had the night before. She was rather surprised to realize that it was going to be just the two of them tonight. Because it was a Friday evening and a race weekend, the restaurant was crowded, but Wade must have called ahead. They were seated after only a very brief wait.

"I thought the others would be joining us again," she said when Wade held a chair for her at the table for two.

"Disappointed?" He waited until she was seated, then took the chair across from her.

"No, of course not." It wasn't that she minded dining with Wade, of course. They had certainly shared many meals together. But maybe it would have been a little more comfortable if they'd had company this evening.

The restaurant specialized in seafood and Lisa wasn't at all surprised when Wade ordered fried butterfly shrimp. Fried shrimp was his favorite meal, one of the many bits of trivia she remembered about their time together. She wondered if he remembered enough about her to have predicted that she would choose the grilled salmon. For all she knew, such details had long ago slipped his mind.

Silence fell between them after the waiter left with their orders. Lisa made an effort to fill it before it grew too awkward. "You must be very pleased about Jake taking the pole for Sunday's race."

"Of course."

"Do you think there's a good chance that both Jake and Ronnie will make The Chase?"

"Yeah, I do. If Ronnie finishes well Sunday—and if some of the other marginal drivers fall to the back."

She arched an eyebrow. "Lots of 'ifs' in there."

"That's racing."

"And you still love it."

"No sense denying it."

"I hope Ronnie finishes well this weekend. I like Katie a lot."

"Yeah, she's nice. And I want Ronnie to do well, too. Just not better than Jake."

"That's a given, of course." She reached for a crab-stuffed mushroom from the appetizer tray he had ordered. "Katie's having an ultrasound next week. They're hoping to find out if the baby's a boy or a girl."

"Yeah?" He selected a bacon-wrapped scallop and popped it into his mouth.

"It's kind of funny. Ronnie wants a girl and Katie sort of hopes it's a boy. But she said neither one of them would be disappointed either way."

"Mmm." Wade reached for the appetizer tray again, and she decided that maybe he wasn't interested in talking about babies. She wasn't either, she assured herself. She had simply been trying to start an innocuous conversation about mutual friends.

So, as always, it was back to racing. "What's your schedule like for tomorrow?"

"Hectic. Inspections, practice, media and sponsor appearances."

Wade had never been much of a talker, but he seemed even more terse than usual tonight. "Wade, is there something on your mind?"

He lowered the mushroom he'd been raising to his mouth. "What do you mean?"

"You seem distracted. I know it's a race weekend and you like to stay focused, but, I don't know. Something seems different tonight."

He shrugged. "I've been thinking about that guy who got shot. The one you work with back in Chicago?"

"Joe Engler? What about him?"

"It could have been you."

That took her aback. He'd been worrying about that? Something that hadn't even happened? "But it wasn't me. I got out of town just after the threats started, remember?"

"What about the next time some disgruntled crook you put away wants to get even? Or some angry and vindictive family member? Remember all those attacks against federal judges in recent years? And several lawyers have been targeted outside of the courtroom."

"I've heard about those incidents, of course, but they really are rare, Wade. I take sensible precautions. I live in a good neighborhood, vary my routes to work, stay alert when I'm out by myself. I've taken self-defense courses and attended several seminars about staying safe. But that's the most I'm willing to do. I refuse to live my life in fear."

"Still, your job does come with some risks, just because of the type of people you deal with every day."

"I suppose there's a slight risk to being a prosecutor, but that's hardly a reason for me to quit. Would you advise Jake to stop driving just because of the danger inherent in his career? You've got to admit that he's much more likely to be hurt on the job than I am."

"Well, yeah, but he's—"

She scowled. "What? A man?"

"That isn't what I meant."

"Then, what?"

"I was going to say that you have the choice to go into other, less risky practices of law. Your father has a whole team of lawyers. You could take over his legal dealings. Or if you don't want to work for Woody, there are plenty of prestigious firms that would be delighted to have you join them."

"I've had this conversation a few dozen times with

my father. I'll tell you the same thing I always tell him. I'm doing what I want to do, for now. I needed to make a life for myself, Wade, apart from my father. Now that my mother's health is so precarious, I'm considering looking for a job closer to home, but it isn't because I'm afraid to stay where I am now or because I want a more so-called prestigious position. I'll probably still be a prosecutor, wherever I end up. It's what I do."

"But it isn't all you're trained to do," he argued. "You would still be practicing law even in those other positions. Isn't that what you wanted?"

"Let me put it this way. Why don't you start driving? You're still young, you could probably get a ride with a start-up team, maybe start racing trucks."

He looked completely baffled by her suggestion. "Why would I want to do that? I'm a crew chief, not a driver."

She lifted her eyebrow in a pointed expression. "It's still racing. And some people would say it's a more prestigious position."

Scowling, he sighed. "Okay. Point taken. Even though I don't think it's exactly the same thing."

Not that he would admit, anyway, she thought in satisfaction. She waited until the server had placed their meals in front of them, refilled their water glasses and left them alone again before trying a new topic. "Have you heard from your brother lately?"

Dipping a large shrimp into a dish of cocktail sauce, Wade nodded. "I saw him in April. He came to the race in Texas and watched from the pits."

"Really?" That rather surprised her, since Wade and

his brother, Harlan, had never been close. She had never even met him during the time she and Wade were together, though Wade had mentioned him in passing a few times.

"Yeah. We've stayed in touch a little more over the past few years. He's married, got a kid now. I guess being a husband and a father made him think a little more about family. Since I'm pretty much all the family he's got, he started calling every couple of months."

"So you're an uncle. Boy or girl?"

"Boy. Thomas Wade. He's four."

And it obviously meant more to him than he let on that his nephew bore his name. "That's nice, Wade. I'm glad to hear that you and Harlan are getting closer. Everyone needs family."

"Yeah? If that's your philosophy, why do you live so far from your own?"

She sighed loudly. "Haven't we been through this already? And I told you, I'm probably moving back to be closer to my folks. I talked to someone in Raleigh a few weeks ago, before the mess with Norris started. I think I can get in there."

"Your parents would like that."

She wondered how Wade felt about the possibility of her living so close again. Not that they would necessarily see each other any more often. And even if they did, they'd been getting along perfectly well during the past few days. Maybe they could be friends, of a sort. She supposed she would like that.

Of course, it would be a lot easier to consider him just a friend if her silly heart would stop fluttering every time his eyes met hers directly across the table. Such as now, for instance.

Quickly lowering her gaze, she stared intently at her plate as she cut into her salmon and hoped he didn't notice that her face had gone suddenly warm again.

"Tell me more about your schedule tomorrow," she said, her voice sounding just a half octave higher than usual to her own ears. "You said you'll be doing some publicity appearances with Jake?"

Apparently making an effort to be more companionable, Wade started talking a little more, giving her an overview of his schedule for the next day, his tone as impersonal as if he were talking to a near stranger. All in all, she supposed that was for the best.

RETURNING TO THE TRACK from dinner, Wade told Lisa he would walk her back to the motor home. It wasn't an offer, she noted wryly, more a statement of intent. She didn't bother to argue with him.

Looking toward the area where the fans parked, she commented on how noisy it was.

He shrugged. "It'll quiet down some when it gets late. Not a lot. Some of the parties go on all night. And they've been known to get a little wild."

Trying to think of something more to say, she cleared her throat and looked up at his motor home. "I hope you aren't too uncomfortable bunking with Jake. I still feel guilty about being in your bed."

Even as the words left her mouth, she wished she had phrased the statement a bit differently.

Wade didn't seem to notice any awkwardness in her wording. "I'm okay at Jake's. Like I said, it's keeping him out of trouble."

"Is that usually a problem?"

"No," he admitted. "Just kidding. Jake isn't easily distracted on a race weekend. He tends to stay in his bus by himself when he doesn't have something scheduled. He watches TV and reads and keeps himself calm and centered. He does his socializing away from the tracks."

Lisa didn't doubt that Jake had all the "socializing" opportunities he desired when he wanted them. Maybe he wasn't exactly her type, but she could definitely see his appeal.

Thinking of her "type" brought her attention to Wade again. He had stopped walking and stood very still, looking at the motor home with a frown.

"What?"

He glanced at her. "Are those yours?"

"Is what mine?" Following his gaze, she spotted the pair of sunglasses lying on the lowest of the steps that led up to the door. "Oh. No, I've never seen that pair before."

"They weren't here when we left."

"So someone dropped them while we were gone," she said with a shrug, trying not to let his tone make her uneasy. "There are a lot of people coming and going around here."

"This area is reserved. We don't usually wander onto each other's steps."

She pushed her hands into the pockets of her jeans

in a nervous gesture. "Maybe someone thought you were there and came looking for you."

"Maybe." But he didn't sound convinced. "I'll come in with you. Look around a little before I head to Jake's."

"You don't think anyone could have gotten inside? Not with the security on that rig?"

"It's highly unlikely," he admitted. "But I'd feel better leaving you tonight if I made sure."

"Okay. If it would make you feel better." She tried to smile. "After all, it's your motor home."

He didn't return the smile. Instead, he keyed in the security code, then entered the coach without waiting for her to precede him. Despite the gravity of the situation, she couldn't help but be a little amused by the way he was acting like some sort of Hollywood bodyguard.

Wade checked every inch of the motor home, even looking in the closet and the shower. Finally convinced that no one was lurking in any hidden cranny, he turned to her. "I guess it's okay."

"I'm sure it's okay. Really, Wade, no one can get into this rolling fortress. And there are too many people around for anyone to risk spending much time trying to break in."

He nodded slowly. "So you won't be nervous staying here tonight by yourself?"

"Of course not. I was perfectly comfortable here last night."

"I could sleep on the couch or something if you…"

"Wade." Smiling, she rested a hand on his arm. "I'm fine. I really don't believe Norris followed me to Pennsylvania, somehow got into the racetrack and then into this reserved area of the infield. I'm sure there's a perfectly innocent explanation for those sunglasses on the steps. But thank you for being concerned for me."

He looked at her hand and then up at her face. Their eyes met. Held. Lisa felt a lump develop in her throat as her heart began to beat too rapidly again. Her gaze slid down to his mouth.

Such a nice mouth, she thought wistfully. Firm and beautifully sculpted. She remembered the way his smiles lifted the right corner just a little, pushing a shallow cleft into his tanned right cheek. Only rarely did he break into a broad, teeth-baring grin, but when he did, the effect was devastating.

As for the way he kissed…well, she remembered that, too. Suffice it to say, he knew exactly how to use those nicely shaped lips.

"Lees?" His voice was suddenly rough, a little gravelly and she suspected she wasn't the only one struggling with inconvenient memories.

She cleared her throat. "Yes?"

"Don't wander off by yourself tomorrow. If you want to get out, call me. Or Katie. I know she'd enjoy spending time with you again."

She wasn't sure what she'd been expecting, but it wasn't that. She dropped her hand to her side. "I can watch out for myself."

"I know. Just humor me, okay?"

"I'll be careful." That was the most she was willing to concede.

Because he had no other choice, he had to be satisfied with that. "I'll keep my cell phone turned on if you need me for anything."

She nodded and moved to one side to allow him access to the door. "Good night, Wade."

He hesitated just long enough to make her wonder if there was something else he wanted to say—or do. But then he moved toward the door. "Good night. Sleep well."

That didn't seem likely at the moment, since she was suddenly so wired she couldn't imagine sleeping at all that night. But since that was a thought better kept to herself, it seemed wiser just to say nothing at all.

CHAPTER SIX

LISA HAD INTENDED to stay inside Saturday, out of the way and out of trouble, but it was an absolutely beautiful day, despite being warm enough to almost make the air sizzle. The draw of the action outside was just too strong.

Maybe it was a subtle way of defying Wade, but she didn't bother to call for an escort before she left the motor home. Why would she? There was no one here who meant her any harm, she assured herself as she made her way carefully through the crowds who were already headed for the stands.

Wearing her security pass on a lanyard around her neck, she headed for the garages. She wouldn't get in Wade's way, she promised herself. She wouldn't even try to catch his eye. She just wanted to watch for a while.

"Hey, Lisa. Good morning."

She turned her head with a smile, recognizing Jake's voice over the racket of voices, car engines and the public address system. "Good morning."

Jake was already dressed in his striking purple and silver fire suit, the Vaughan Tools logo splashed prominently across his chest and his many other sponsors promoted on his sleeves. He looked like a walking billboard, but a very attractive one. Good looks weren't a requirement for a NASCAR driver, but it certainly didn't hurt when one was this photogenic, she thought, noticing the women watching him appreciatively from outside the secured area.

"Where's your entourage?" she asked as he fell into step beside her toward the garage. She had to almost shout for him to hear her. The noise coming from the cars still parked in the garages was almost deafening.

She knew he was usually surrounded by people on race weekends—her father had mentioned that Jake had a personal assistant, who also handled public relations duties and whose primary job was to keep Jake on schedule. There were so many obligations involved with being a NASCAR NEXTEL Cup driver, in addition to actually driving the car. She suspected he had a full slate that day and was surprised that he hadn't already gotten started.

Jake leaned his head close to hers so she could hear him reply. "I gave them the slip an hour ago. I had a headache starting and needed to take a pill and chill for a while. Pam's been paging me like crazy, but I told her I'd be back in time for the next scheduled function, and I am. I'm a few minutes early, actually."

"What do you have scheduled?"

He shrugged. "One of my sponsors has a couple of VIPs they want me to meet and schmooze. You know, shake hands, pose for pictures, flash my PR smile."

He accompanied the words with a broad, glittering grin that made a couple of passing women sigh audibly, and Lisa couldn't help smiling in response. Anyone else might have come across as cocky, but Jake was so charming and so wryly aware of his own manufactured and packaged image that it was impossible not to like him.

She knew he had his share of "haters." There were plenty of fans of other drivers who resented Jake's media popularity, not to mention his impressive record of besting their drivers on the track. Wade had told her once that having "haters" was the sure sign of a champion driver. It was much better to be greeted with cheers and boos upon arrival at the track than with disinterested silence, he had assured her.

Someone bumped into her on the crowded walkway, and Jake reached out immediately to steady her. "You okay?"

"Yes, thank you."

His arm remained lightly around her shoulders as he guided her through the throngs. "Should you really be wandering around out here by yourself? I know you don't want to go the bodyguard route, but maybe you should have an escort when you mingle with the crowds."

"I don't need an escort," she assured him, as she had Wade the night before. "I feel perfectly safe here."

As if to reinforce her words, a uniformed track security guard passed them, nodding recognition to Jake and giving a cursory glance at Lisa's pass. A camera flash went off somewhere nearby, and Lisa frowned. She had hoped to stay low during this weekend, not calling undue attention to herself as Woody's daughter. Having eligible bachelor Jake Hinson's arm around her, no matter how innocently, was no way to stay out of the limelight.

Maybe she should have stayed in the motor home, after all.

Jake seemed to sense the direction her thoughts had taken. "Sorry," he said, dipping his head close to hers again. "I know you're trying not to call attention to yourself. I guess I shouldn't have joined you."

"Don't worry about it, Jake," she said, turning her face toward him and away from the curious onlookers. "I doubt that anyone knows who I am. My father's publicity hasn't included me or my mother—deliberately, on his part. Besides," she added teasingly, "no one's going to be looking at me when your pretty face is nearby."

He groaned and rolled his eyes. "If you're trying to flirt with me, forget it. I don't want Ice knocking my helmet off—with my head still in it."

Even though she knew he was joking about her flirting with him, the rest of his statement made her eyebrows rise. Surely he wasn't implying that Wade would be jealous if she flirted with Jake? Jake hadn't even known them when Lisa and Wade were together, and they had made it very clear that there was nothing but friendship between them now.

"Don't be silly," she said.

His grin was crooked. "Think I'm joking? Maybe you should look to your left."

Following his suggestion, she spotted Wade headed their way, wearing a scowl that would probably have frightened small children out of his path, had there been any. She could see why Jake might mistake that glare for jealousy, but she was sure there was another reason entirely for Wade's disgruntled expression.

Maybe something had gone wrong in the garage. The car was the only thing that was important to him on practice day.

He spoke in a bark. "Jake. Don't you have someplace to be? Pam's been pacing a path around the hauler waiting for you."

Jake apparently knew Wade too well to take offense at his curt tone. Instead, his face lit with a mischievous grin and his arm tightened around Lisa's shoulders.

"Guess I'd better go mingle with my admirers," he said, making sure his voice carried clearly to his crew chief. "Thanks for showing me such a great time, Gorgeous."

Giving her a conspiratorial wink as he leaned closer, he brushed his lips lightly across Lisa's cheek, then turned and walked away. Leaving her, she thought wryly, to face Mr. Grumpy alone.

"Lisa."

"Wade," she said gravely.

He glanced in the direction of Jake's disappearing back. "You and Jake seem to be getting along well."

No way was he really jealous, Lisa reminded herself. He was just grouchy. "I ran into him on the way here. He said he'd been battling a headache this morning."

"Allergies," Wade said with a slight shrug. "Chronic condition."

"Will it affect his driving?"

"Jake doesn't let anything interfere with his driving."

Oddly enough, it sounded as though there was a message embedded in that statement. A warning to her? Surely not.

Wade glanced at his watch. "I've got some things to do."

"Then don't let me hold you up. I thought I'd roam around, check out the souvenir booths and sponsor exhibits."

"By yourself?" He shook his head. "Not a good idea. Let me take you to Katie. I saw her over by their hauler."

"I don't need you to take me—"

"Lees." He took her arm impatiently. "I've got enough to worry about today. Don't add yourself to the list."

He really was grumpy today. Maybe he was always like this at the track. She wouldn't really know, since he'd never let her hang around with him there before. Reminding herself of her promise that she wouldn't interfere with his responsibilities this weekend, she allowed him to escort her to Katie, though she had to hide her irritation with his bossiness.

"DAMN IT, VINCE, watch what you're doing!"

"Sorry, Ice."

Wade winced in response to the surprise he heard in the crew member's apology. He knew he'd been unusually irritable during practice, and the fact that it hadn't gone as well as they had hoped wasn't much of an excuse.

They'd had plenty of lousy practices before. Heck, last year Jake had plowed into a wall during a session, forcing them to go to a backup car and start at the back of the field for the race the next day, despite having qualified third. Even then, Wade had lived up to his nickname and kept his emotions in check.

Yet he was having a hard time not snapping at everyone who walked past him. And his sneaky suspicion that seeing Jake's arm around Lisa had instigated his bad mood didn't make it better. His urge to punch Jake when he'd kissed Lisa had given him even more grounds for concern.

He shouldn't have invited her here. But since he had, he shouldn't have let his old feelings for her affect his thinking.

Even when they were engaged he'd had the sense to keep her away from his work, knowing that his concentration was endangered when she was around. And now, almost six years after they'd gone their separate ways, he was no more immune to her than he had been before.

It wasn't going to be easy smiling and glad-handing at the media events he and Jake had scheduled that afternoon. A taped TV appearance and a joint interview for a racing magazine had been set up in the media center during the time the NASCAR Busch race was taking place at the racetrack. Somehow Wade had to pretend that there was nothing on his mind except tomorrow's race.

Striding toward the hauler, he had to pause to allow a line of small children to cross in front of him, being herded by a couple of women he knew to be involved with the family outreach program. Some of the kids looked kind of familiar; maybe he'd seen them around with their driver dad or crew member parents. He couldn't be sure, since he didn't pay that much attention to kids when he was at the track, but he'd attended a few barbecues and parties where people brought their families.

It wouldn't be long before Ronnie and Katie's kid was ripping and romping with the rest of them, he realized with a bemused shake of his head. And maybe another one soon after that, if Katie had her way.

It seemed like everyone in the business had a family these days. Wives, kids, dogs. He wasn't sure how they pulled it off. Racing was a demanding business, involving long hours, very few days off and an oppressive amount of traveling.

True, those demands were sometimes too challenging to overcome and plenty of unions hadn't survived the obstacles, yet he could name quite a few long-time successful marriages among his racing associates. He would bet that Katie and Ronnie would be among them.

Moving on toward the hauler when the kids were out of the way, Wade recalled something Jake had said recently about marriage. Jake had confessed that he rather envied Ronnie, who was so palpably happy with his bride. Jake made no secret of wanting a family someday, though he was admittedly being extremely selective about potential partners. So far he hadn't found anyone with whom he wanted to make that momentous commitment.

When Jake asked Wade if he had ever considered

marriage again after the end of his unsuccessful engagement, Wade had merely shrugged and said he didn't consider himself the marrying kind. He was too wrapped up in his job, he figured.

He hadn't added that he suspected he was too reserved and emotionally guarded to give any woman—especially one like Lisa—what she needed. His dysfunctional family had taught him to keep his feelings and vulnerabilities to himself, a deeply ingrained habit he didn't know how to overcome at this stage.

He had tried with Lisa. He'd fallen in love with her almost the moment he'd first laid eyes on her and he'd convinced himself that he could make it work with her. That he could somehow be different for her. Yet he'd been braced for failure from the beginning, so he wasn't overly surprised when she told him with tormented eyes and quivering lips that she couldn't marry him. That she had decided to pursue a life of her own, one that didn't include him.

He had been devastated, though he thought he'd done a good job of hiding the extent of his disappointment from Lisa. From everyone.

He'd salvaged what remained of his pride by throwing himself into his work, rising even more quickly through the ranks of Woodrow Racing, justifying that advancement with a string of successes that ensured he would have a job there for as long as he chose to stay. Though he'd considered working for someone other than the man who might have been his father-in-law after Lisa dumped him, he'd stayed with Woody out of loyalty and affection. Woody had rewarded him by making him a crew chief, Wade's most cherished hope.

Since the breakup, Wade had poured all his passion, all his emotion, into racing. He wasn't sure he had anything more to give.

He had been secretly aware of the hole Lisa left inside of him when she walked away, which he'd tried to fill with even more work and more determination to take his driver to the top. But he'd learned to accept the possibility that there would always be an emptiness somewhere inside him, no matter how many championships ended up on his resume.

There was a part of himself that would never get over losing her. But that was a part that no one— especially Lisa—would ever get the chance to see, he vowed.

In the meantime, he thought as he reached for the door to the hauler, he had a job to do. And he intended to do it even as he kept Lisa safe until she could return to the life she'd left him for.

LISA HADN'T HAD SO much fun in a long time. Maybe she had been working too hard these past few years, she mused. Maybe she really had needed a vacation, though she certainly wouldn't have chosen to take it for this reason. Or maybe Katie just knew how to show a visitor a good time.

They had watched the practice together, and then Katie had taken Lisa around to meet her closest friends among the other wives and girlfriends. They had gossiped with the women, played with children, passed around babies and overindulged in homemade snacks. And laughed. She couldn't remember the last time she laughed so much.

Most of the women she met led active lives of their own, careers or charitable causes to which they gave their time and skills. She suspected there were others like her mother, who contentedly found their identities through their husbands, but those weren't the ones Katie hung out with.

They had barbecue for dinner that evening, cooked on a huge grill set up beside the hauler. She learned that many of the teams enjoyed cooking at the track, turning it into a competition of sorts for who could prepare the best trackside food. In their case, Bubba Doohan, the hauler driver, and Tony Holmes, Ronnie's hauler driver, collaborated to serve tender ribs dripping with barbecue sauce, corn on the cob roasted over the flames, fresh coleslaw and even dessert—cherry cobbler.

Wade, Digger, Jake and Ronnie ate together, their knees almost touching as they juggled plates in their lawn chairs and put away an impressive amount of food while carrying on a serious-looking conversation. No doubt talking about the race tomorrow, Lisa thought, sitting in a lawn chair next to Katie.

Other members of the two crews drifted by in clumps, talking, filling plates, then carrying them away to find a relatively quiet place to eat. There were other grills at the other haulers parked closely together in the area, and all of them were surrounded by people who were tired and hungry after a long day of preparations. Out in the infield, dozens of other grills and smokers were being put to use in the fan RV areas and the air was filled with the scents of cooking meat mingling with the other track aromas—beer, exhaust fumes, sweat and burned rubber being among those that Lisa could most easily identify.

She had noticed that the mood among the various crews seemed to be changing as race day drew closer. Expressions were more serious, conversations more intense. There was still a lot of joking and laughing, but there was no doubt that these people were here to do a job and that they took that job seriously.

Even between the Woodrow Racing teams, as friendly as they were, the spirit of competition was evident. Each team wanted a win, their eyes were on the points chase. They might be friends and coworkers out of their cars, but on the track and in the pits, they were fierce rivals and no one forgot that.

She found herself looking forward to the race more than she had even expected. It would have been difficult to hang around the track for this long without getting caught up in the spirit of the event. She was going to watch from the top of the hauler, and Wade had even promised to get her a headset so that she could hear what was being said between himself, Jake and the spotter during the race.

Her loyalties were a bit torn, actually. She had grown so fond of Katie and she knew her new friend hoped Ronnie would win. But Wade had been so generous in offering Lisa his motor home and his protection that she really wanted to see a win by the Number 82 car as a reward for Wade's kindness. She hadn't gotten as close to the members of the other two Woodrow teams, but she knew her father would be pleased by a win by any of his drivers.

She finished her ribs and delicately licked the sauce off her fingers, following the example of everyone around her. Finishing the cleanup job with a paper napkin, she glanced across the way and found Wade watching her. For some reason, he was scowling as though she'd done something to irritate him. She lifted her eyebrows at him in question, but he merely shook his head and turned back to listen to something Jake was saying.

"Lisa, did you hear me?"

Lisa turned to Katie. "I'm sorry, I guess I zoned out for a minute. What did you say?"

Looking rather knowingly from Lisa to Wade and back again, Katie repeated, "Do you want to join us for Bunko tonight? One of our usuals isn't here this week and everyone said you're welcome to fill in."

"That's very nice, but I don't know how to play."

With a dismissive wave of her hand, Katie assured her that didn't matter. "It's super easy. Hardly takes any skill at all. But the game doesn't really matter. The point is just getting together and being silly and having a good time with the girls."

All of which sounded so nice after the stress and anxiety of the past couple of weeks. "I'd love to join you, if no one minds."

"Don't be silly. We're always on the lookout for fresh gossip. We'll get you tipsy on cheap wine and then ask really inappropriate questions about your personal life. It'll be fun."

Though Lisa laughed, as Katie had intended, she made a vow to herself to go easy on the "cheap wine" that evening.

CHAPTER SEVEN

NEARLY EVERYONE KNEW ABOUT the weekly Bunko game Katie's group of friends participated in. No men were allowed, so Wade couldn't tell for sure what went on, but rumor had it that things got kind of wild. A bit too much wine, lots of risqué jokes, some cheerful male-bashing. All on the pretext of playing a game that apparently involved a lot of dice and few rules.

Wade didn't blame Katie and her friends for needing a weekly retreat from the stress and testosterone of the racing circuit. While more women were becoming involved in the sport, there were still a lot more men than women behind the scenes. The wives and girlfriends sometimes felt neglected and superfluous, and he could certainly understand that. He was all for any activity that gave them a break from the relentless demands on their families' time and energies.

Which didn't mean he was entirely comfortable knowing Lisa was among them this evening. He tried to tell himself he was simply concerned for her safety, but he knew even as the excuse crossed his mind that it wouldn't fly. She was safe enough with Katie. He just didn't like the thought that the others might be grilling her about her former—and purported present—relationship with him.

He made a point to hang around the meeting room the women had reserved for their game when it was time for the party to break up. It was getting late and there were several things he could be attending to on the night before the race. He knew Jake was already in his motor home, resting and relaxing, getting focused and prepared for the early start to tomorrow's grueling schedule. And yet he still managed to be on the spot when Lisa and Katie stepped outside together.

"Ladies," he said, moving to stand in front of them.

They were smiling ear to ear, slightly flushed and disheveled. He noticed that Lisa had a tiny smudge of chocolate at the corner of her mouth and Katie had a smear of what might have been cheese dip on her blouse. Lisa's eyes looked a little too bright, her steps just a little unsteady, giving him a clue to what had gone on during the game party.

Their smiles froze a bit when he appeared, and to his suspicious eyes they looked oddly guilty for a moment. He couldn't help wondering if they had talked about him at some point during the evening. Or was he just being paranoid?

"Have a good time?" he asked in what could only be described as a drawl, even by him.

They exchanged quick glances before Katie replied, "We had a very nice time."

"Lovely time," Lisa echoed.

Katie nodded vigorously. "Great game."

"Fun game," Lisa agreed.

"Good food."

"Great food."

"And maybe a little booze?" Wade inquired politely.

"Just a little wine," Lisa said, sounding defensive.

"Not for me, of course," Katie said with a shrug. "I drank sparkling grape juice. And Lisa just had enough wine to let her relax a little."

"I wasn't criticizing. Just asking."

"So why are you here, Wade?" Katie asked. "Were you looking for Lisa?"

"I thought I could escort you both back to the motor homes. Since it's so late," he added awkwardly.

Both Katie and Lisa looked surprised. He wasn't sure why. Lisa, especially, should understand why he would be concerned about her.

Though they were in an area restricted to racing insiders, they could hear the bursts of noise coming from the infield parking area crammed with so many motor homes and fans on hand for the next day's race. Despite the security of the track, he couldn't help but be concerned that it would be possible for someone who didn't belong to somehow slip in among the crowds.

It would be even more of a concern the next day, when thousands more spectators would arrive, filling the hundred-thousand-plus seats. He intended to make sure that he knew where Lisa was every minute tomorrow, though he was going to try his hardest to keep his concern for her from interfering with his work.

Because that sounded so improbable even to him, he

decided to forget about tomorrow for now and concentrate on seeing Lisa safely to the motor home.

He escorted both women through the maze of coaches that served as a mobile community for the racing families, dropping Katie off at her home first. The lights were on inside and they could hear the TV playing as Ronnie relaxed for tomorrow's events. Watching Katie go inside after exchanging warm good-nights with Lisa, Wade knew she would be happily welcomed by her adoring husband.

He hoped Ronnie performed well tomorrow. Though not quite as well as Jake, of course.

"Every time we do this I feel guilty," Lisa murmured when Wade keyed in the security code to his motor home. "I should have stayed in a motel."

Wade sighed and shook his head. "How many times are we going to have this conversation? I'm fine bunking on Jake's couch for a couple of nights. He doesn't mind, and I'm not there that long, anyway. I'm usually up and out by five every morning."

"But—"

"Lisa," he interrupted firmly, "drop it, okay?"

She frowned, but complied.

Opening the door for her, he said, "I need to come inside to grab a few things out of my closet. I'll only be a couple of minutes."

"Sure." She moved up the steps as she spoke, stumbling a little on the top riser.

Wade caught her arm. "You okay?"

"Of course," she said with an embarrassed laugh.

"I guess I shouldn't try talking and walking at the same time."

"Not after being plied with wine by Katie's Bunko group," Wade agreed, tongue-in-cheek.

Lisa glared at him and dropped onto the couch. "Don't let me stop you from getting what you need," she said pointedly.

Chuckling, he moved into the bedroom and opened the door to the walk-in closet. It was a bit jarring to see Lisa's clothes hanging in there beside his own. There was something unsettlingly intimate about the sight of her shirt nestled up to one of his.

Calling himself an idiot, he grabbed items with more haste than planning, stuffing them into a tote bag and hoping he had everything he would need the next day. Walking out of the closet, he found himself looking directly at the big bed that dominated the bedroom.

It wasn't hard to picture two heads snuggled cozily into his thick, comfy pillows, a mental image that had probably been suggested by seeing those two shirts in his closet. Whatever had inspired the thought, it ade him scowl as he rejoined Lisa, firmly closing the bedroom door behind him.

She was still sitting on the couch where he'd left her. Leaning back into the cushions, she had her eyes closed. A half-smile tilted the corners of her unpainted lips. He stopped in his tracks, unable to look away from her sweetly contented face.

He had never forgotten how beautiful she was, but he'd learned long ago how to block the memories from his mind when they'd crept up to haunt him. He wondered how long it was going to take him after this to learn to do so again.

She opened her eyes and smiled sleepily up at him. "Find everything you need?"

A whole list of inappropriate responses scrolled through his mind before he said lamely, "Uh. Yeah."

When he didn't immediately move toward the door, she lifted an eyebrow. "Was there something else?"

Nothing more than his intense reluctance to leave, he admitted silently. He really should be on his way, before he did something stupid. Such as...

"You have chocolate on your face."

"Really?" She lifted a hand to the wrong side, scrubbing futilely at her cheek.

"No." He took a step toward her, setting his tote bag on the coffee table. "It's here."

She went very still as he leaned over her, lightly rubbing his fingertip next to the left corner of her mouth. Her skin was so soft. A little warmer than usual, whether because of the wine or the flush that now colored her cheeks, he couldn't say.

The lipstick she'd worn earlier had all worn off, leaving her mouth bare and vulnerable, her lips showing a tendency to quiver in response to his touch. Which, of course, made it impossible to resist running his fingertip across them again.

"Wade," she murmured, her lips moving against his skin.

He swallowed a groan, telling himself to get out of

there now. Before he did something even more foolish. Such as...

He lowered his mouth to hers.

MAYBE LISA HAD BEEN just a bit tipsy when she'd left the Bunko party, but she sobered up abruptly the moment Wade's lips touched hers. This was not a good idea, she told herself firmly—even as she reached out to grab his shirt collar with both hands.

Almost six years had passed since they had last kissed. And yet when it came to this, nothing seemed to have changed. His slightest touch could still make her tremble with excitement and hunger. His kiss still had the power to make her forget every stern warning she had ever given herself about him. Every attempt she had made to stop loving him.

Loving him? She drew back with a sudden gasp, breaking the contact between them. "Wade—"

He straightened immediately. "Sorry. I've never been able to resist the taste of chocolate."

The joking comment didn't match the almost grim expression in his eyes, but she was grateful for the lifeline he threw her as she floundered. "Yeah, well, find your own dessert," she said, forcing a short laugh.

He didn't smile, but he turned toward the door, snatching up his tote bag on the way past. "I'll send someone to get you in the morning," he said. "We'll have lunch at the hauler, then you can watch the race from the top. I don't want you alone at any point tomorrow."

She was too tired and bemused to even bristle at his

bossy tone. She figured she would do what felt right the next day without necessarily consulting Wade about it. But there was no need to argue about it tonight.

It was much better if he simply left—despite some recalcitrant and utterly foolish part of her that wanted him not to go at all.

LISA HADN'T FULLY realized how many responsibilities a team had on the day of a race. Especially the driver and crew chief, who had to deal with the fans and media in addition to all of their other responsibilities. Jake and Wade seemed to go from one interview or sponsored appearance to the next, answering the same questions over and over, signing a hand-cramping number of autographs—Jake more than Wade, in that case—posing for pictures and still somehow attending to the business of racing.

From a safe distance, but always surrounded by members of the team, she watched the proceedings, fascinated by the activities and rituals. She attended the nondenominational worship service for the racing families, listened in at the drivers' meeting in which NASCAR officials reminded everyone of the rules and regulations for the race and watched as fans vied for attention from their favorite drivers.

There was even a small grandstand between the garages and pit road where fans with pit passes could wait for drivers to walk by and then hand items such as hats, shirts and photographs through holes in the fence for autographs. The drivers seemed to accept that avid gauntlet as part of the day's program, graciously pausing every few steps to scrawl their names on whatever was offered to them.

In the grandstands, at the many concessions and souvenir stands and on the tops of buses and motor homes in the infield, the tens of thousands of fans were pumped and ready for the day's event. They were loud, excited, enthusiastic in their cheers and jeers when the racers were announced. Lisa still found it disconcerting to hear the boos—it seemed so rude—but it was all part of the sport, and the drivers seemed to view it as such.

She could certainly see the appeal of those drivers in their colorful firesuits, their helmets tucked beneath their arms as they swaggered to their cars. No women driving this time, she noted with a sigh, but she had spotted a few in the garage. Progress was made a few steps—or, in this case, laps—at a time.

It was an impressive sight to see all the teams in their matching uniforms lined up for the invocation and the national anthem. A lump actually formed in her throat when the Air Force jets did their noisy flyby overhead. The lump grew larger when she saw Wade in his purple and silver uniform and sporty sunglasses, headset in place, a look of intense concentration on his good-looking face.

Forget the drivers, she thought with a sigh. She seemed to have a thing for crew chiefs—one, in particular.

Wade would work from his seat on top of the pit box, where he could see everything that went on in the pit and had access to a computer for figuring everything from lap times to gas mileage. She hadn't expected to sit close to him during the race; that would be too distracting for him. At least, she wanted to think so.

"Miz Woodrow?" A tall, painfully thin man swathed in team colors approached her with a headset as she sat on top of the hauler in a chair topped by an umbrella to protect her from the sun. "Ice wanted me to make sure you had these so you could hear the action. He told me to make sure they're working okay and to tell you, er, not to leave the hauler unless someone goes with you.

"Don't know why," he added in a mutter, "It ain't like the track's a dangerous place to be."

She couldn't help smiling. "Wade has a slight tendency to be overcontrolling. And overprotective."

The man, whose name tag read J.R., nodded energetically. "Comes from being the boss of so many people, I guess. There's, like, fifty people who answer to him. Got a lot of responsibility on his shoulders. Good man, though," he added. "I think the world of him."

Sliding her headset into place, Lisa murmured, "So do I, actually. Thank you, J.R., I'll be fine now if you need to get back to work."

"You just give a signal if you need anything, you hear? If you get too hot out here, you can watch the race on the plasma screen in the hauler lounge. And if you get hungry, there's soft drinks and snacks in the kitchen. I'll bring something up for you or you can just go down and help yourself—long as you don't wander off too far and get Wade all nervous."

The grin he gave her as he added the condition was one she couldn't help returning.

She had dressed coolly enough for the heat, and the umbrella over her chair provided her with enough shade for comfort, so she chose to watch from where she was for now. The transporter was a huge, two-level semi-trailer that carried both the primary and back-up cars to the racetracks on the top level. The pneumatic lift for the vehicles remained up during the races to provide an awning for the opening to the back of the hauler.

In addition to carrying everything from cars to pit box to uniforms and tools, the hauler served as the team office at the track. It was fitted with a refrigerator, microwave and cabinets full of food, crew lockers, and the lounge area with leather wraparound couch, a built-in desk for a computer and phone and a plasma TV complete with a full range of audio visual equipment and Jake's favorite video game system.

From where she sat high above the concrete, she could watch everything in the pits below her, as well as having a view of the busy garage area and the crowded spectator stands. Jake's spotter, whom she knew only by first name, Arnie, stood high atop the stands with the other spotters, giving him an unimpeded view of the action. Arnie would be responsible for keeping Jake out of trouble on the track. He would monitor every minute of the action through binoculars, communicating warnings of any potential trouble to Jake, whose peripheral vision was limited in his protective, high-back, wraparound seat.

Some nonfans probably thought the driver was isolated out there in his car, but the truth was, he was in almost constant communication with his spotter and crew chief. It was up to Jake to let Wade know how the car was running, whether it was too tight or too loose, how it responded in traffic or clean air, in curves and on straightaways. Wade's job at that point was to relay instructions to the pit, who would make every effort to improve the vehicle's handling by making adjustments.

It still amazed her that the well-practiced and perfectly-coordinated pit crew could change four tires, fill the tank, clean the windshield and make minor handling adjustments in under fourteen seconds. It took her almost that long to unscrew the cap on her gas tank.

After being given the famous command, forty-three engines started simultaneously, the noise so loud that it was nearly deafening even through her headset. The smell of exhaust blended with the scents of food, beer and sweat, and would soon be permeated with a burnt-rubber tang. Lisa knew that particular blend was the finest perfume to the noses of the most rabid racing fans.

And then the cars were moving, following the pace car around the uniquely triangular track in a parade of colors and numbers and sponsors' logos. Leaning forward in her seat, she felt her pulse rate increase and sensed the mounting excitement of the crowd. The pace car exited to pit road, the green flag waved and the race was on, forty-three massive engines roaring like attacking lions.

LISA HAD HEARD non-race fans say they couldn't imagine how anyone could watch a bunch of cars going around in circles for four hours or more on a Sunday afternoon. She, herself, usually had work in front of her when she watched the races on TV, looking up from the computer only when the announcers excitedly pointed out something happening on the track. But actually being at the track…well, that was an entirely different experience.

There was so much to see, so much activity all around her. The noise seemed to vibrate inside her chest, and it was almost dizzying to try to follow the cars around their circuits. She was fascinated.

It was particularly interesting to hear the conversations going on through her headset. Jake, she discovered quickly, tended to get overexcited when he was racing. The car wasn't handling as well as he liked at the beginning and he was losing positions, falling back to the twelfth spot, even after a couple of pit stops made under cautions.

He was almost collected in a Turn Two wreck on lap twenty-two and another on lap forty-four. Both times he had his spotter to thank for keeping him out of danger, both near misses getting him even more perturbed.

If she hadn't already known, Lisa would have found out then how Wade had earned his nickname. The more tense Jake became, the more soothing Wade's voice became, his steady, soothing influence having an obvious effect on his driver.

Wade kept reassuring Jake that the crew would soon

have the car exactly right, that Jake was doing an amazing job, that he had no doubt a great finish was practically guaranteed. And it worked. By the time the race was more than two-thirds finished, the car was handling beautifully and Jake had stopped complaining and was focusing fiercely on catching the leaders.

Engine blowouts were becoming an issue toward the end, as Jake had predicted. Cars that had been in serious contention went out not with a crash, but with a stomach-sinking billow of smoke from beneath the hood. She could see the stress on the faces of the crews in the pits as they willed their cars' engines to take the abuse just a little longer.

Lisa was on her feet, along with the other hundred-thousand-plus spectators, as the race neared its conclusion. Jake had made his way to the seventh spot and was closing in fast on the cars ahead of him. Though she wasn't sure he had enough time to pass them all, it seemed to be a good bet that he would finish in the top five, a very satisfactory performance.

Someone got loose and hit the wall in Turn Two, taking two other cars with him in a noisy, metal-crunching crash. Lisa grimaced, covering her mouth with unsteady hands as she watched to make sure no one was hurt.

Two of the crumpled cars headed straight for pit road, letting her know that the drivers were chagrined, but uninjured. The most badly damaged car wasn't going anywhere without a tow truck, but the driver put his window net down, signaling that he was okay. He was assisted from his vehicle and taken directly to the infield care center for the mandatory post-wreck evaluation, but Lisa could tell that he was more angry and disappointed than hurt.

She turned her attention back to Jake. Wade had instructed him to come in for a pit stop during the caution, having predicted correctly that all the other lead cars would do the same. And then, he warned Jake to stay within the mandated pit road speed. A speeding penalty at this point would be disastrous.

Never was the pit crew more invaluable than during these end-of-the-race stops. Lisa watched as the over-the-wall members stood poised for Jake to come to a stop, their muscular bodies almost visibly vibrating in their colorful fire-retardant uniforms, their grim faces mostly obscured by protective helmets.

This was what they practiced endlessly back at the shop, filming themselves going through these motions and then scrutinizing the tapes and trying to do even better next time. Pit stops were exhaustively, painstakingly orchestrated. The tiniest misstep, the extra hundredth of a second could be the difference between a win and a loss at the finish line.

The instant Jake was in the pit, they were on him, swarming the car like efficient purple and silver robots. After a quick debate between taking four fresh tires or two, Wade had decided to go with right-side only, a surprisingly risky call since most of the other leaders were taking four. It said a great deal for Jake's confidence in his crew chief that he accepted the gamble with little argument.

A NASCAR official hovered over them, making sure

every lug nut was firmly in place, every required "*T*" crossed, and then Jake was away in a squeal of tires, Wade yelling at him to watch his speed.

Pleased with their timing, the pit crew high-fived and slapped each other on the shoulders before turning to watch the rest of the race, tension evident in the set of their shoulders. They weren't questioning their leader's gutsy call, but they were all clearly worried about the two older tires.

Wade's decision had gotten them the track position they wanted. First out of the pits, Jake reentered the race in third position behind two drivers who had decided not to pit at all during the caution—equally daring moves since it had been a while since either had been in for fuel and fresh tires. Behind Jake were several fast cars with four fresh tires.

It was going to take every ounce of skill he possessed to stay ahead of them. Crossing her fingers, Lisa held her hands to her chest, feeling her heart pounding against her ribs.

CHAPTER EIGHT

REMEMBERING THAT HER FATHER had three other cars in the race, Lisa quickly checked their positions during the final caution lap. Ronnie was now in eighth place. Not bad. Mike was a lap down following an earlier incident, somewhere around the twentieth position.

The rookie, Scott, was farther behind, having been collected in one of those early wrecks and being off the track for a number of laps while his car had been repaired. Still, barring more problems, he would complete the race, which was always better than a DNF (did not finish) on his season record.

Having done her duty toward the other Woodrow Racing drivers, she concentrated again on Jake's team, her gaze turning to the purple pit box on which Wade sat leaning forward, staring fiercely at the track. A reporter stood on the ground beneath him, microphone held up toward Wade's mouth, questioning him about his decision to take two tires. He seemed to be answering cordially enough, but she could see by his body language that he was impatient for the reporter to go away and let him pay full attention to his driver.

The pace car left the track, the green flag fell and

engines screamed as pedals hit metal. Jake went low, as did the Number 53 behind him, both of them passing the second-place driver, who had faltered on the restart. And then it was a battle between the Number 82 and the Number 53 cars for second position as they advanced relentlessly on the leader.

Once again an edge of anxiety crept into Jake's voice over the headset, and once again, Wade was unruffled. "No worries, Jake," he drawled. "We're looking good. You can pull ahead on Turn Three."

Standing next to Lisa for the end, J.R. shook his head and chuckled. "That's why we call him Ice," he shouted to Lisa over the noise surrounding them. "Ain't nothing that bothers him."

She wondered if she was the only one who detected the faintest changes in Wade's voice. As unperturbed as he sounded, it was still obvious to her how important this was to him, how badly he wanted a win. And how heavily the responsibility weighed on him to make that happen.

Ice? Maybe on the outside. But she still believed Wade had a great deal of emotion inside that he refused to allow anyone to see. While the skill served him well in his role as crew chief, it was also a strong defense mechanism he used to protect himself—and a daunting deterrent to anyone who wanted to know him intimately.

Her heart nearly stopped when Jake tried to make a pass on the leader and almost got loose. She thought she might have screamed a little when his back end fish-tailed just a bit, but the sound was lost in the pandemonium around her. The Number 53 car almost got around him, but Jake managed to block, keeping his second-place position. In the headset, the spotter was yelling, as was Jake, but Wade continued to be the voice of calm.

Jake had his car under control again now. Second place with five laps to go and a car with four fresh tires right on his rear bumper. Wade cautioned Jake repeatedly to keep his head, to stay in command.

The sounds of hard impact drew everyone's attention to Turn One, where two cars had collided, spun out of control and caused several other cars to wreck along with them. Lisa winced when she saw that Ronnie was one of the drivers caught up in that melee. He'd simply had nowhere to go but into the side of another car, despite the best efforts of his frantic spotter. Knowing Katie would be disappointed, Lisa shook her head sadly.

Because NASCAR always tried to finish under green for the sake of the fans who loved a heart-stopping ending, there would be one attempt for a green-white-checkered finish. After the caution, one lap would be completed under green flag, one under the white one-to-go flag and then the checkered flag would fall, signaling the end of the race. A shoot-out, some called it, with every driver giving it his all to finish in the best position possible.

Through her headset, everyone was talking so fast that Lisa had trouble keeping up, though Wade's was the voice she listened to most closely. There was such confidence in his measured tone that it almost seemed that Jake was guaranteed the win. She could hear Jake taking reassurance from his crew chief's quiet confidence, a new sense of resolve sounding in his own voice.

The pace car fell away. On his four worn tires, the lead driver slid up the track on the restart, and both the Number 82 and the Number 53 cars took immediate advantage of the opening, dropping low and rocketing around him. Jake had taken the lead.

Lisa's heart was pounding again now, her hands clenching so tightly in front of her that her knuckles hurt. Still she couldn't seem to loosen her grip. The crowd roared, almost drowning out the near-deafening car engines.

The Number 53 car dropped low, taking a look around Jake's car. Jake blocked frantically, weaving to take up as much track as possible. Turn Two—and Jake almost got loose again, the back of his car slipping just enough to make Lisa gasp, along with the other thousands of spectators riveted to the action. She knew everyone was questioning the two-tire call now and that Wade would be the one to take the flack if it proved to be a mistake.

She heard the spotter shouting instructions, Jake yelling back and then Wade's voice, deep, calming, encouraging, despite the pressure he must be feeling. Jake shot forward again, keeping the Number 53 car behind him.

Lisa didn't realize she was cheering until she ran out of breath. When Jake inched a little farther ahead, she started chanting again, "Go, go, go, go, *go!*"

Beside her, she could sense that J.R. was jumping up and down and bellowing, but she didn't take her eyes off the track long enough to look at him. She wasn't even watching Wade then. All her concentration was on that purple and silver car, as if she could help Jake hold the lead through willpower alone.

Jake crossed the finish line a tenth of a second ahead of his rival. And promptly lost his left rear tire. The ring of worn rubber shot away from the wheel, bouncing onto the apron and across the grass as if celebrating its hard-won victory.

"*Whooo!*" Wade startled her by shouting into the headset, letting his emotions show for that one glorious moment. "Way to go, Jake! You're the *man!*"

Lisa laughed, delighted by the pure elation in Wade's voice.

Jake was hollering, thanking Wade, thanking his crew and laughingly announcing that he was heading straight for Victory Lane. There would be no celebratory spins today, he announced wryly. It would just be too embarrassing to hit the wall during a victory celebration.

Lisa realized that her throat was sore. She'd gotten so carried away at the end of the race that she'd almost screamed herself hoarse.

No wonder people became addicted to this sport, she thought, dazedly shaking her head.

She would have loved to have gone to Victory Lane to join Jake and Wade, but they had agreed ahead of time that, should Jake win, it would be better if she remained in the background. If the media realized that Woody's daughter was here for this victory, someone would be sure to ask for a comment, and she was still trying to remain somewhat inconspicuous.

With J.R.'s assistance, she climbed down the two-level ladder to the pavement below. She didn't expect Wade to be waiting for her at the bottom.

She stared up at him, seeing the satisfaction in his face, the high color that was just starting to recede a little from his cheeks. For Wade, that was quite a show of emotion. "I thought you would be with Jake."

"I'm on my way there now," he said, his voice still characteristically calm. "Just wanted to make sure you're okay. You'll stay here at the hauler until I get back?"

She looked longingly after the crew, who were already dashing to join their driver. "I'd like to walk around a little, maybe watch some of the action in Victory Lane."

Wade shook his head. "Too many people milling around over there right now. I think it would be better if you hang out here. Unless you want me to try to find you an escort…."

Knowing he needed to hurry to join Jake, she shook her head. "I'll wait here," she conceded reluctantly.

"Thanks. I'll try to hurry."

"No. Take all the time you need. Now go. You deserve your time in the spotlight. That was an amazing race you pulled off today. You and Jake both."

Wade startled her by reaching out to give her a quick hug—just a squeeze of the shoulders, really, but enough to make her heart stutter. And then he was gone, running to join his team. She was surprised he had hung around long enough to speak to her; she would have thought she'd be the last thing on his mind right now.

Still feeling the warmth of his arm around her shoulders, she went into the lounge of the hauler. She would wait here for Wade, quietly out of his way.

That sobering thought drained a great deal of her exuberance over Jake's win, leaving her frowning as she turned on the TV to watch the post-race commentary.

"IT'S GETTING KIND OF LATE," Wade said as he parked in front of Lisa's parents' house Sunday evening. "Think your folks are still up?"

Glancing at the lights burning in the windows, she nodded. "They tend to turn in early, but not quite this early. There's a TV show Mom likes that comes on at nine on Sunday evenings. I'd bet she's watching that. Dad's probably still in his office, gloating about Jake's win, making lists of all the calls he's going to make tomorrow and preparing for the review meetings with his team leaders."

Sounding wryly amused, he said, "You seem to know their schedule pretty well."

"I should. It hasn't changed for as far back as I remember. Mom enjoys reading and watching her TV shows and there's nothing Dad would rather be doing than working. I know it was hard for him to miss being at the racetrack today, feeling like he was calling all the shots for all four teams."

Wade turned in the driver's seat to look at her, and she wondered what he had heard in her voice. "He's been spending more time with her since she's been ill, you know."

Unlike her? She wondered if there was an implied

criticism in his comment or if she was simply reading too much into it. "You don't have to convince me that my father loves my mother, Wade. I'm aware of that. He would be devastated if anything happened to her."

"Yes. They seem to be happy together."

"This is all Dad's ever wanted," she said with a slight shrug. "A palatial home, a loving wife, a successful business that lets him have the means to indulge his passion for racing. He would have liked to have had a son, but they weren't able to have more children, so he settled for being a hands-on, rather paternal owner for you and Digger and Jake and Ronnie and all the other hundreds of people who work for Woodrow Racing."

"He's very proud of you, you know. He thinks you've accomplished a great deal."

"My father likes to pretend law school was his idea, even though you and I both know he would be perfectly happy for me to come back home and let him take care of me for the rest of his life."

"Woody just wants you to be happy. And safe. He doesn't know why you couldn't be living closer to home and putting your law degree to work for him. You know he has a whole fleet of attorneys on retainer. I'm sure he would happily turn that part of the business over to you."

"Yes, well…" She reached for her door handle. "It's been an interesting weekend, Wade. Thank you for letting me be a part of it."

His hand fell on her forearm, detaining her. "What are you going to do now?"

"Now?"

He shook his head impatiently. "I don't mean this minute. I mean now that we're back from Pennsylvania. Will you be staying close to home here? You aren't planning to go back to Chicago yet, right?"

"Not just yet. I still have three weeks left of my leave and my boss thinks I should take all of it, despite the heavy workload I've left behind. I think he knows I've been considering moving closer to my parents, and he's giving me a chance to think about that decision. I'm sure he's looking around for potential replacements while I'm gone."

"How does that make you feel?"

She shrugged. "Kind of funny. I've enjoyed working there. I have a lot of friends there. But I can make new friends in a new job. I'd still be doing the same work."

"So you're staying with prosecution, despite everything that's happened to you."

"Nothing has actually happened to me," she reminded him. "I'm just being cautious."

"For good reason. You have a coworker who was shot."

"A very rare occurrence."

He shook his head. "What does it take to scare you?"

There were several potential answers to that question. Because all of them had to do with him, she decided she'd better leave it as rhetorical.

"You're coming in, aren't you?" she asked, instead. She motioned toward the security gate through which he had driven only minutes earlier. "They already know we're here. Dad's probably expecting you to come in and gloat with him about today's win."

Wade glanced at the house. As usual, there was little expression on his face, but she thought she saw the faintest signs of uncharacteristic nervousness in his eyes. Why would Wade suddenly be uncomfortable about talking to her father? Especially tonight?

"Yeah, sure," he said, opening his door. "I'll walk you in. Just let me get your bags out of the trunk."

With a bag in each hand, he followed her up the front steps. They paused simultaneously at the door, Wade waiting for her to reach for the doorknob. Instead, she turned to look up at him.

It had occurred to her suddenly that when she opened this door, the weekend would be officially over. And for some reason, she was reluctant to turn the knob.

She believed she recognized that same reluctance in Wade's eyes. And she thought she saw something else— something that made her hands start to tremble.

He stood very close to her. So close that it would take only a step to bring her up against him. One very small step, and she would be in his arms. Which was exactly where she wanted most to be at that moment.

Maybe he saw her thoughts reflected in her face. His eyes darkened in the artificial glow of the porch lights. "Lisa—"

"Yes?"

"Open the door."

"I will." But rather than turning, she stood where she was, still gazing up at him.

Since his hands were full, he couldn't open the door himself without dropping one of her bags. He frowned. "What are you waiting for? Your parents are probably wondering what's keeping us out here."

"Probably." She couldn't resist reaching out, laying a hand on his chest, so temptingly close. She was gratified to feel his heart racing beneath her palm, to know that she wasn't the only one affected by this moment.

The rhythm of his breathing changed, becoming a bit ragged and uneven. Still, he was so controlled that she wouldn't even have known had she not been standing so close to him. Touching him.

What would it take, she wondered, to make Wade McClellan finally, completely lose control? It had never happened while they'd been together before, not even during moments of passion. He'd certainly held himself in check when she'd broken up with him.

Even during the race, when things had looked the worse for Jake, Wade had been totally collected. Sure, he'd cheered when Jake won. She'd watched on the TV in the hauler as he and Jake high-fived and celebrated in Victory Lane, being sprayed with champagne and a sponsor's soft drink. He'd been jubilant, no doubt about that. But he'd shown nothing he didn't want exhibited to the public.

Ice.

And yet…

She could feel his heart pounding against his ribs, belying the studiedly cool expression on his face. And when she glanced down, she saw that the knuckles of both his hands were bone-white from the tight grip he had on her bags. Not quite as unaffected as he pretended to be.

Intrigued, she moved a half step closer to him.

"Lisa—" Her name was almost a groan that time. Wade wasn't nearly as cool as he wanted her to believe. And that she found almost irresistible.

"I just want to thank you once more before we go in."

"Not necessary."

"No. But I want to. Thank you, Wade." Just because she wanted to feel his reaction, she tiptoed and brushed her lips against his. And she was rewarded when his heart gave another hard thump against his ribs. Against the hand she had pressed over it.

Her bags hit the porch with a thump. The next thing she knew, his arms were around her and his mouth was on hers. And his wasn't the only heart pounding frantically.

He was still in control, she thought dazedly, but his emotions were much closer to the surface than they usually were. Given a little more time, she might just be able to push him over...

Because she wasn't sure she was prepared for that, she pulled away from him, breaking the kiss with a little gasp. "I guess we'd better go in," she whispered.

His hands on her upper arms, he looked down at her and for a moment she thought he was going to kiss her again. She knew if he did, all her caution would be forgotten.

Then he nodded, released his grip on her and stepped

back. "Let's go in," he said, picking up her bags, his composure firmly back in place.

LISA WASN'T PARTICULARLY surprised when her father rushed Wade off to his office almost as soon as they walked in—or as close to rushing as he could get while still using a walker. Visibly pleased with the outcome of the day's race, Woody couldn't wait to sit down and rehash the race lap-by-lap with his crew chief, even though Ellen chided him to wait until the next day, after Wade had gotten the chance to rest from the exhausting day.

"Don't keep him too late," she called after the men when she lost the argument. "He's tired, Woody. He'll be back tomorrow."

She shook her head in resignation when she and her daughter were alone in the den. "I just know he'll keep the poor boy talking half the night. You wouldn't believe how excited your daddy was when Jake won that race this afternoon. I watched with him. He was so worried that Jake would crash like poor Ronnie did."

"Dad really wants that championship, doesn't he?"

"It's something he's been working toward for the past twenty years. Ever since he bought his first race car and started building his teams, he's wanted a championship. He's come so close, having drivers finish second in points four times now, but that big trophy has always eluded him. Now, this year, with Jake and Ronnie both doing so well and Mike not far behind..."

"He has a chance."

Her mother nodded. "Exactly."

"And if he does get the championship?"

Laughing, Ellen shook her head. "He'll start craving a second one."

"I understand the fascination with racing—especially after spending a weekend in the middle of the action—but I really don't get the obsession." Lisa made a frustrated gesture with one hand. "There are so many other things in life. Family. Travel. Theater."

"None of which you've had time to indulge in since you started your job in Chicago," Ellen murmured.

Lisa cleared her throat. "I've been busy. Establishing my career."

"Hmm."

"But I still plan to take full advantage of everything life has to offer once I'm solidly entrenched somewhere," she insisted. "I don't want to be so narrowly focused on my job that I can't even see anything or anyone else around me."

"Are you talking about your father now—or someone else?"

Feeling her cheeks warm in response to her mother's perceptive tone, Lisa looked down at her hands. "I'm talking about everyone who's so obsessed with career that nothing else matters."

"I take it your weekend with Wade didn't go well?"

"No, it was fine. I had a very nice time."

"You didn't see Wade much?"

"I saw him quite a bit. He bunked with Jake while I stayed in the motor home, but we had several meals together and were usually within sight of each other."

"So he didn't ignore you?"

"No, he didn't ignore me."

"Yet he was still able to concentrate on his work enough to help Jake win the race."

"Yes."

"So the problem was…?"

Reminding herself that she had to be careful not to reveal too much of her career predicament to her worry-prone mother—not to mention her overreactive father—Lisa smiled and shook her head. "No real problem. As I said, I had a great time. It's nice that Wade and I are able to be friends again."

"Just friends?"

Trying not to think about that unsettling interlude on the front porch, she shrugged. "For now. Probably for good. I'm not sure we're any more suited for each other now than we were before. But…" she added, carefully keeping the cover story alive, "there's always a chance, I guess."

Her mom looked at her oddly, and Lisa could tell she wasn't being entirely successful in selling the story she and Wade had concocted. Maybe she should just come clean and tell the whole truth, somehow figuring out a way to reassure her worried parents that she was taking the necessary precautions to keep herself safe.

She opened her mouth to do just that, but was interrupted by the impatient thump-thumping of her father's walker. He came into the room looking quite satisfied. "Wade said to tell y'all good night. He'll be back tomorrow afternoon for a meeting with all the team leaders.

You'll probably want to ask him to join us for dinner, Lisa."

"Oh, I—"

"Great weekend for you to go to the track, wasn't it? That was a heck of a win Jake and Wade pulled off. Guess I was wrong about you being a distraction. Looks like you were more of a good-luck charm."

"Dad, I—"

"I can almost taste that championship," her father gloated, his green eyes glittering beneath his heavy gray brows. "If it weren't for this stupid hip replacement, everything would be just about perfect right now, wouldn't it, Ellie?"

Ellen smiled indulgently and nodded. It was typical of her not to mention her own health problems, just as it was typical of Woody not to acknowledge them. Not because he didn't care—he did, a great deal. He simply refused to accept the reality that her health was precarious.

Because Lisa accepted that frightening fact all too well, she bit back the confession she'd been about to make, telling herself there was no harm in waiting until Norris had been recaptured and any possibility of danger was over before giving her parents the facts. Wade was a willing coconspirator for now, so maybe it was just better to leave everything alone until the time was right.

She pushed herself out of her chair. "I'm really tired. I think I'll turn in. I'll see you both at breakfast, okay?"

Her dad chuckled, still basking in the high of Jake's win. "Got to get your beauty sleep, eh? Gonna be seeing Wade again tomorrow."

Giving him what felt like a somewhat sickly smile in response, Lisa left the room. She felt her mother watching her as she walked out, but she didn't look back. She was more than ready to be alone for a while.

CHAPTER NINE

SOMEHOW WADE ENDED UP having dinner with Lisa and her family Monday evening. He wasn't sure whose idea it had been, but Woody was the one who had extended the invitation. Wade wasn't oblivious to the fact that Woody had decided he approved of a reunion between Wade and Lisa. The old schemer had done everything but nudge them into each other's arms that evening.

Wade wasn't overly flattered by the implied approval. He had known Woody long enough to understand how the older man's mind worked. Especially now that Jake's team was performing so well, Woody had an eye on the future.

Woody knew Wade had been approached a few times by other owners wanting him to help them rebuild struggling teams or take over for people who had been wooed to other organizations. He knew Wade's loyalties lay solidly with Woodrow Racing, but he'd probably like to guarantee that loyalty literally by making Wade part of the family.

Woody wasn't so much looking for a son-in-law, Wade thought wryly. He had his eye on a lifetime employee.

Wade couldn't help wondering if Lisa was as aware

as he was of her father's machinations. Probably. Woody wasn't all that hard to read.

He wondered what Lisa thought about the blatant matchmaking. He couldn't tell from looking at her expression across the dining table.

There had been a time when he'd thought he read her pretty well. He'd realized how wrong he'd been about that on the night she had broken their engagement. He'd been taken completely unaware that night. He had been pleased about the approaching wedding and he had blindly assumed she felt the same way.

She had told him she loved him. But then she'd told him she didn't want to be his wife. And the cozy, comfortable future he had envisioned for them—he building championship race teams, Lisa waiting contentedly at home for him—had all disintegrated around him.

He should have known better than to think a guy like him could make Lisa happy. Maybe if she was a different kind of woman, one who would be satisfied with the money and fame and excitement that was part of racing...but then she wouldn't be Lisa. She deserved more. More than he knew how to offer.

Even if she had kissed him like she still wanted him. A kiss that had kept him awake long into the night, wondering exactly what she'd meant by it, if anything more than the simple gratitude she had implied.

Two conversations were taking place at the table. Lisa and Ellen chatted about Lisa's experiences in Pennsylvania, the friends she had made there, the fun she'd had with Katie and the others. Woody, of course, wanted to talk about the race, itself, replaying almost all the calls Wade had made and the pit strategies that had helped Jake get up in front. They had already been over all this, last night and again during the meetings earlier that afternoon, but there was nothing Woody would rather talk about.

Eventually the two conversations merged, with Lisa telling her parents about her experiences during the race— a topic that interested her father. There was laughter as she described J.R.'s overeager catering to her needs during the event, and Wade grinned because he was the one who'd asked J.R. to make sure she had everything she needed.

She brought to life the tension in the pits when Jake had almost been collected in the early crashes and during those final laps when his tires had become an issue. She was a good storyteller, and her parents responded warmly to their only offspring's chatter.

It was nice being part of a family dinner for an evening, Wade mused. Despite Woody's workaholic nature and his tendency to ignore his wife and daughter at times during the past, Wade had no doubt that there had been many lively dinnertime conversations among this little group. They were close, in their own way.

He couldn't help thinking back to his own family. He could remember only a handful of times they'd actually sat down together for a meal. His mother hadn't liked to cook and had rarely been home in the evenings, spending most of her time hanging out with her friends in bars and bingo parlors. His father had also been in bars and casinos, with a different group of buddies.

From the time they were old enough to fend for themselves—younger than most children were deemed ready for that responsibility—Wade and his brother had been on their own at mealtimes, making do with sandwiches and cereal for the most part. Growing tired of cold food, Wade had finally taught himself to cook. Spaghetti with canned sauce had been his specialty, but he'd also learned to grill meats and boil vegetables. He and Harlan had eaten fairly well through high school, usually on trays in front of the TV.

One might think they'd have grown close during those years spent pretty much raising themselves. Instead, they had drifted into different crowds, different interests, until the McClellan family was nothing more than four virtual strangers who occasionally crossed paths in the same house.

He wasn't sure what had kept his parents together. Convenience, probably. The financial advantages of two incomes. Neither of them having to take full responsibility for the sons they had conceived for no logical reason. The last time he remembered being with both his parents at one time had been his high school graduation, which they had attended in separate vehicles so they could all go off with their own friends afterward.

A week later, Wade had moved out, determined to make a place for himself in the racing world. He'd rarely gone back, even though his parents still lived in that same empty-feeling house. If they would have liked to see him more than they did, they'd never told him.

As for him and his brother, well, it was kind of nice

that they had finally established a relationship, of sorts, but they would never be truly close. After only four years of working together, he and Jake were tighter now than he and Harlan would ever be. And as for a father-figure…he looked toward the end of the table where Woody sat beaming as Lisa described the thrilling end to the race.

Wade had once thought he could become a part of this family. A son to Woody and Ellen, husband to their daughter, father of their grandchildren. It hadn't been the primary reason he had wanted to marry Lisa, but there had been a definite appeal to the side benefits. He should have realized that his past had left him totally unprepared to join a family, much less to start one of his own.

"You're being awful quiet tonight, Wade," Woody announced with his typical lack of tact. "Something on your mind?"

"Woody," Ellen murmured.

Wade forced a smile. "Just enjoying this delicious meal," he said. "Virginia, you've outdone yourself tonight."

Having just entered the room with a tray full of desserts, the housekeeper beamed. "Thank you, Mr. Wade. I'm glad you liked it."

He happened to glance across the table then to find Lisa watching him a bit too closely. She must have sensed that there was more to his distraction than culinary appreciation. He gave her a quick, bland smile and turned his attention to the generous slice of pie à la mode Virginia had just set in front of him. Maybe he was only a visitor at this table for an evening, but he could certainly enjoy every moment while he was here.

THEY HARDLY HAD TIME TO MOVE into the den after dinner when Woody announced that he and Ellen were going to retire to the master suite to watch a television program they both enjoyed before turning in early. "You kids can visit down here for as long as you like," he added as he all but hustled his wife out of the room. "We won't be back down tonight."

Rather stunned, Lisa gazed toward the doorway through which her parents had just disappeared. She hadn't even had the chance to say good-night.

She turned slowly toward Wade, who was standing close behind her, staring in the same direction. He looked at her—and he grinned. And then they were both laughing. It felt so good to hear his rare, full-throated laughter.

"I'm sorry," she said, shaking her head. "Dad's not exactly the most subtle guy around."

"Your father makes a steamroller look subtle. But he's a great guy. He means well."

"I know." She sighed and tucked a strand of hair behind her ear. "He's decided what's best for me again. And now he's trying to make sure it happens."

"Us, you mean."

She nodded. "He's been dropping hints ever since I got home."

"He sees it as a way to bring you back for good."

A little embarrassed, she nodded. "I guess. I haven't told my parents I'm looking into positions closer to home. I wouldn't want them to be disappointed if it doesn't work out."

"And you haven't told them yet about the threats to you in Chicago?"

"No. I'm still not ready to tell them yet. Not until I'm confident there's nothing for them to worry about."

"So as far as your dad knows, you'll be going back to Chicago in a couple of weeks, rested and ready to stay there for a while. No wonder he's looking for any excuse to keep you here."

Was that how Wade saw himself? As a tool to be used by Woody—for managing his racing team, for racking up wins, for keeping his daughter in line?

She shrugged, keeping her tone light. "Dad's very fond of you, you know. He would probably adopt you if he thought it would keep you in his organization. He's not so much using you to keep me here as he is using me to make you a part of the family."

What might have been just a touch of pink appeared for a moment on Wade's cheeks, and Lisa found that fascinating. She had seen him uncomfortable before, but she'd never seen him blush. What had embarrassed him? Her saying that her father was fond of him or her allusion to her dad's renewed goal of a marriage between them?

He pushed his hands into his pockets. "So, what are you going to do this coming weekend? Are you staying here or going with me to Indianapolis? Or have you decided yet?"

She kept her hands clasped in front of her to prevent

herself from wringing them. "It fits our cover story better if I go with you, of course."

He nodded. If he had a preference either way, he kept it carefully hidden.

"I'd probably be perfectly safe here."

"Probably," he agreed with a shrug. "And it shouldn't be too difficult for you to keep the whole truth from your parents."

Which, of course, made her worry that her parents would extract the whole story from her, especially her mother, who'd always been the hardest one to fool. "I've never been to the Indianapolis track," she said.

"So come with me. I think you'll enjoy it. It's a completely different atmosphere from Pennsylvania."

"I'd like to come, but only if I can stay in a hotel. I won't take your motor home again. It isn't fair to you or to Jake. Maybe Dad hasn't given up his reservation in Indiana yet. I can stay in the room he always books."

Wade frowned. "You'd be safer in the motor home. If you stay in a hotel, you'll have to travel back and forth from the track, outside the security gates. Your dad spends most of his time in the garages and the hauler office, just going to the hotel to sleep. You're going to want a place to crash during the days I'm busy."

"I won't take your bed again."

"We'll work something out, okay? Assuming you decide to go, that is."

She nodded. "Then I'd like to go—if it isn't too much trouble for you."

"We'll make it work," he said again.

She searched his face for doubts about the wisdom of her spending another weekend with him, but his thoughts were closed to her. "So, it's decided."

He nodded. "I'll make the arrangements. You can be the one to try to keep your dad from booking a church for the wedding once he finds out you're traveling with me again."

Though her cheeks warmed a little, she kept her tone light when she replied, "I think I can handle that part."

"SO YOU'LL BE AT THE Indianapolis race? Girl, I am so jealous."

Holding her phone loosely to her ear on Wednesday afternoon, Lisa smiled faintly. "When this is all over and my life gets back to normal, I promise I'll get you tickets for the Chicago race next year. VIP tickets," she added, making a mental note to hit up her father for that favor.

Davida had been such a lifeline to her, letting her know everything that was going on back in Chicago while keeping Lisa's confidence about her location and her family connections. This was the least she could do to repay her.

"You don't have to do that," Davida said, but the excitement in her voice at the very possibility made Lisa even more determined to follow through. "That package you sent me yesterday was generous enough. I'm so thrilled with the T-shirts and caps and mugs and autographed hero cards you sent me."

Lisa had put together a package of Woodrow Racing memorabilia along with the autographs she'd collected in Pennsylvania and had sent the gifts by overnight courier to Davida on Monday. She knew her friend would be delighted with the delivery and would be discreet about where the items had come from.

"I'm glad you liked the stuff," she said lightly.

"Are you kidding? I'm using my Jake Hinson coffee mug as we speak."

"Good." She changed the subject. "I'm glad to know that Joe's out of the hospital and doing well. I was really concerned about him."

"He's going to be fine. Especially now that he's finally agreed to accept protection until Norris is recaptured."

"And there haven't been any other incidences since Joe was shot?"

"No, nothing. Not even another threatening letter or phone call. Norris is either laying low or maybe he's given up and left the area."

Lisa wasn't enthusiastic about either of those possibilities. She wouldn't feel entirely safe until she knew Norris was securely behind bars again. She certainly didn't want him to hurt anyone else, but he needed to come out into the open again for the authorities to find him.

"You'll let me know if there are any other developments?"

"Of course. Didn't I promise I would?"

"Yes. Sorry, I just get so impatient at times for this to be over."

"Even though you're on your first long vacation… well, ever…and you're getting to hang out in the racing world? That's got to be more fun than working."

"It would be even more fun if it were my idea."

"Well, yeah, I can see that," Davida admitted, growing somber now. "But seriously, Lisa, try to have a good time, okay? And maybe Norris will be brought in pretty soon and you'll be able to come back home."

Home. The word made Lisa frown. She didn't really think of Chicago as home. Rather as the place where she lived and worked between visits home. "I just hope they find the S.O.B."

Davida chuckled. "That's the spirit. So I'll talk to you soon, okay? And I hope your dad's drivers do well again this weekend."

Promising to pass along the sentiment, Lisa disconnected the call.

WADE COULDN'T STOP pacing. He had almost worn a path into the wood floors of his house by midnight Wednesday.

He should be sleeping. He'd be leaving early the next day for Indianapolis. He and Lisa. Which probably explained his pacing.

Ever since he'd talked her into accompanying him to Indianapolis, he had been asking himself why he'd been so determined to convince her. For her safety? Kind of hard to convince even himself of that since she was probably safer in her father's well-secured mansion, much farther away from Chicago than Indianapolis.

To protect her parents from the truth? Somewhat more believable, since she had expressed concerns about how they would take the knowledge that their daughter had been targeted by a dangerous criminal. He worried about that, himself. So he was helping her keep it quiet, right?

Nice try. But he suspected the real truth was that he simply wanted her with him again. As inconvenient as it had been at Pocono, in some ways, he had enjoyed having her there. Knowing she was around to talk to him, to dine with him, to support him in his work.

It had been exactly what he'd envisioned when he'd asked her to marry him all those years ago—though he wouldn't have pictured them staying in separate places at night. He thought of those shirts entangled in his closet, the two pillows side-by-side on the big bed in his motor home, and he was forced to clear his throat. Hard.

He definitely hadn't hoped for separate sleeping quarters.

He spun on one heel, pacing again in the opposite direction through the downstairs of his rather ordinary three-bedroom house in Mooresville. His steps weren't impeded by much furniture. His home was decorated in a minimalist style, little more than the necessities filling the good-sized rooms.

With stock car racing having become such a popular and successful sport, most of the drivers and an increasing number of the well-compensated crew chiefs lived in palatial estates, often on the shores of nearby Lake Norman. Without a family to draw him home, Wade tended to spend almost all his time at the shop and in the garages, so that it had seemed unnecessary to pour too much energy into decorating the house where he spent so little time. That line of reasoning had made it much easier for him to justify the expense of his motor home and the driver he employed for it.

As he prowled through his house now, he found himself looking at it through a different perspective. How would Lisa react to it? Accustomed to her father's wealth and a lifetime of the luxuries he had provided for her, would she see his home as stark and unappealing? She had talked about living modestly in Chicago on a prosecutor's salary, but she'd always known she could go back to luxury if she'd wanted.

He made a lot more money now than he had when they'd been engaged. Woody compensated him very well for the hours, the sacrifices, the successes they had achieved together. He supposed he could provide a McMansion for a wife if he had one. If she wanted that sort of thing. He could support a family in decent style, though the time he would have to offer them would certainly be at a premium.

Which brought him back to the reason he and Lisa had split up in the first place. As much as he enjoyed having her as his moral-supporter during the past weekend, it wasn't at all the life she wanted. She didn't need to be pampered or provided for. Not by her father and not by him. She had a satisfying career of her own, and it wasn't one that would allow her to spend most of her time on the road with him, even if she wanted to.

He thought of his own parents, living their separate lives, practically strangers to each other on the rare occasions when their paths crossed. That wasn't what he wanted from a marriage, and he doubted that Lisa would be satisfied with such an empty union.

The attraction was still there. On both their parts, judging by the way she had kissed him on her parents' doorstep. But it took more than attraction to hold a long-term relationship together, especially in his world. The fact that he loved her—always had, always would— didn't mean they could hold a marriage together.

Maybe he'd deliberately resisted seeing that obvious truth six years ago. He knew better now.

He would have to be very careful in Indianapolis. More guarded than usual around her.

He was grimly aware of the fear that motivated that line of thinking. He even acknowledged the irony. While he might be willing to take risks at the track without blinking, he was darned near terrified of letting himself get too close to Lisa again.

There were those who said his nickname suited him very well. That his heart really was made of ice. But Wade was all too keenly aware that even solid ice could be shattered by a hard enough blow.

FOLDING CLOTHING into a suitcase early Thursday morning, Lisa tried not to look too uncomfortable beneath her mother's thoughtful gaze. Her mom sat on the edge of the bed, ostensibly to keep her company as she packed, but not doing a very good job of hiding the concern she felt.

"Lisa, are you absolutely sure there's nothing you want to talk about?"

Lisa pushed her makeup case into one corner of the suitcase. "Like what, Mom?" she asked too casually.

Her mother frowned at her, reminding Lisa all too vividly of the rare times in her childhood when she'd tried to hide anything from her too-perceptive mother. She had almost never succeeded. She wasn't sure she'd gotten any better at it with age.

"Something's been bothering you ever since you got home from Chicago," Ellen said bluntly. "I don't know if it's Wade, or if it's something to do with your job, but I just feel like you're worried about something. I wish you would confide in me. Maybe there's nothing I can do to help, but it might help to talk about it."

Guilt stabbing through her, Lisa cleared her throat. She didn't want to lie to her mother, but she wasn't ready to tell her everything yet, either. She focused on the least dangerous of her troubles—physically, at least. "I suppose I do have some concerns about whether I should be accompanying Wade this weekend."

"Why is that?"

Adding her curling iron to the suitcase, Lisa answered slowly and completely candidly, "I'm a little afraid of falling for him again."

"I thought that was the whole point of you traveling with him. To see if there's still a spark?"

Which edged toward dangerous territory again. And, again, she was able to be honest in her answer without mentioning the problems in Chicago.

"I wanted to get a closer look at the sport that totally consumed the two most important men in my life," she said quietly, sitting on the bed beside her mother. "My father—and my fiancé. I never felt as important to either of them as racing was. Is."

"Oh, honey."

Lisa held up a hand and shook her head. "I never watched a race while I was in law school, never told anyone about my connection to the sport. Even when I moved to Chicago, I kept Dad's identity quiet. Only one of my friends there is aware of it. But then I started watching again, trying to understand. And I have to admit, I was drawn in. I became a closet fan, watching all the time, keeping up with Dad's team, especially Wade and Jake."

"Your father would be pleased to know that."

"He's already been surprised, I think, that I've known so much about how the season's been going so far."

"Pleasantly surprised. He thought you hated racing."

"I did, for a while. I guess I thought of racing as a rival, taking the two men I loved away from me. But then I grew up and I saw it for what it is. A sport. A pleasant diversion for many people, an obsession for others. I can enjoy it without completely understanding the obsession."

"I hope you realize now that your father has always loved you."

"Yes, I know. He just has his own way of showing that love—by pampering and protecting and sheltering. It works for him. And for you, obviously," she added gently.

Her mom smiled wistfully. "But not for you. Because you're exactly like him."

Lisa chuckled wryly. "Maybe I am. Maybe that's

why I couldn't hate racing forever, no matter how much it has cost me over the years."

"That's a good thing, you know. Someday the team will be yours and you'll have to make the decision whether to sell it or run it yourself."

Lisa felt her smile turn shaky. "I don't want that to happen any time soon. I expect Dad to be around micromanaging Woodrow Racing for a very long time."

"He will be," her mother predicted confidently.

"In the meantime, I wish you could talk him out of trying to marry me off to a racing insider just so he'll have someone to run the team when he retires."

Ellen laughed at that. "I can't talk your father into anything, Lisa. You should know that by now. But finding his replacement isn't the only reason he wants to marry you off to Wade. He's very fond of the boy. And he thinks it would bring you home for good. As far as he's concerned, it's a win-win-win situation."

Lisa wondered how Wade would feel about being referred to as "the boy." The rest wouldn't surprise him.

Her mother grew serious then. "I've never felt neglected by your father, you know. I've been very happy being his wife and your mother. I know the life I've chosen isn't the one for you, but I want you to always remember that I've been satisfied. Whatever you decide to do, I want you to be as happy as I've been. Whether it's with Wade or with someone else or on your own, you choose to enjoy the journey, you hear?"

Lisa didn't like the undercurrent she heard in her mother's advice, as if she was leaving these words of wisdom now in case she wasn't around to say them later. But maybe she was just being overanxious. Her mom had always been available to offer advice when solicited. And her most frequent advice concerning happiness was that, except in cases of severe clinical depression, one could choose to be a happy person or an unhappy person.

She had often cited examples of people who remained positive and optimistic even in the face of great obstacles. It was all a matter of attitude, she had said. You could see yourself as a victim or a survivor, a winner or a loser, a positive contributor to society or a negative force in the universe. All very Zen and idealistic, but typical of Ellen. And it had been that advice that had guided Lisa when she'd decided to break her engagement to Wade and pursue a career that would make her feel useful and fulfilled.

She stood and closed her suitcase. "I'm trying to enjoy the journey, Mom. Trying to explore every path available to me. Just like you've always taught me."

Ellen's eyes had turned misty. "You'll choose the right path, sweetheart. I've never doubted it."

Leaning over to kiss her mother's cheek, Lisa murmured, "I love you."

"I love you, too, darling. There's the doorbell. That must be Wade."

A little ripple of anxiety coursed through her, and Lisa wasn't sure if it had more to do with the upcoming trip with Wade or the fear that there would come a time when her mother wouldn't be available for these precious heart-to-heart talks. Still feeling a little guilty that she hadn't shared the full story with Ellen, Lisa grabbed the handle of her suitcase and tried to keep a positive attitude as she moved toward her bedroom doorway.

CHAPTER TEN

WADE HAD TOLD HER that Indianapolis was a different experience than Pennsylvania, but Lisa hadn't realized exactly how different it would be. She'd half expected that one track was pretty much like another. And while that was true as far as physical details—both had grandstands, garages, concessions and souvenir stands—the atmosphere wasn't at all alike.

While the other track's setting had been almost pastoral, there was an edgy, urban feel to the Indianapolis track, the largest sporting venue in America. The two-and-a-half mile oval seemed to stretch forever, and so many more people were packed around it that Lisa's head spun just thinking about the numbers.

This was why people enjoyed traveling the NASCAR circuit in their RVs and campers, she realized, studying the crowds. It wasn't just watching the cars go around and around. It was the whole, unique experience of each race. Sure, some of the drivers and crews were getting a little weary more than twenty weeks into the grueling season—but once the green flag fell, they would be just as fired up as they had been for the season kickoff at Daytona back in February.

Maybe she could understand, a little, how a person could become obsessed.

She had been welcomed back among the crews with a warmth that had pleased her, making her feel as though she'd become one of them. Sure, she was the owner's daughter and that earned her a few perks. And she was with Wade, assumed to be dating him, so that, too, was the basis for some minor kissing-up. But she liked to think that maybe she'd made a few friends on her own, last week.

As if in affirmation of that wish, Katie had greeted Lisa with a crushing hug, a beaming smile and a burst of chatter, as if they had been separated for weeks rather than a few days. Almost in her first breath, she announced that she and Ronnie were having a girl, which of course initiated another hug. And then she went on to talk about everything else that had happened since they'd last seen each other—a surprising amount, considering how little time that had actually been.

They dined together Thursday evening, as they had the week before. Lisa, Wade, Jake, Katie, Ronnie and Digger. Pizza, this time, rather than grilled meats, but the same amount of lively conversation. The men discussed qualifying, the women talked about the baby, though Ronnie kept drifting into the latter conversation. He was so obviously thrilled with the gender of the baby they expected, since he'd made no secret of his desire for a daughter. A boy next time, he said, grinning, but first that little girl.

"Yeah, let's see how you feel about having a daughter when she brings home some yahoo with a ring pierced through his nose and a snake tattooed around his neck," Digger grumbled, apparently from personal experience.

Ronnie scowled. "I don't think so."

"Yeah? How you going to stop her?"

"By locking her in her room, if necessary. I'll let her know which guys she can date—and none of them are going to be race car drivers," he added with a glowering look at Jake.

As the others laughed, Jake held up his hands. "Don't look at me. Thirty years is a little too much of an age difference for my taste."

"Why do I have the feeling my husband and daughter have some heated discussions ahead?" Katie asked Lisa ironically.

"It's a given," Lisa replied, remembering some of the battles between herself and her own ironfisted father during her teen years.

"Do you have a name picked out yet?" Wade asked, looking as though he couldn't think of anything else to contribute to a discussion about children.

"Olivia," Katie and Ronnie answered in almost perfect unison.

"It was my mother's name," Ronnie said. And for Lisa's benefit, added, "She passed away last year."

"She was a very special lady," Katie chimed in. "I was glad to have the chance to know her. And we've chosen Jeanette for a middle name, after my mother. She's so looking forward to her first grandchild."

Lisa smiled at both of the proud parents-to-be. "That's a very pretty name."

It wasn't going to be easy growing up as the child of a driver, she mused as she reached for a second slice of pizza. And she knew this just from the experience of being the daughter of an owner. Olivia's father wouldn't be home for weekend excursions or soccer games or ballet recitals or birthday parties. The family's activities would have to take place on the road, their motor coach as much a home to them as their place in North Carolina. But maybe Ronnie would do a better job of making Olivia feel included than her own dad had with her.

The conversation had moved on, turning back to the upcoming weekend activities. Digger, Ronnie and Jake got into another discussion about qualifying strategies. Katie paid attention to what they were saying as she finished her pizza.

Wade, Lisa noticed, seemed unusually distracted for the remainder of the meal. She wasn't sure whether he was thinking about the race or something else, but he seemed very far away, even though he sat right next to her.

"I DON'T LIKE YOU staying here by yourself," Wade fretted as he drove into the parking lot of the hotel where Lisa would be staying in the suite her father had reserved months earlier for himself. "I'd feel a lot better if you'd just stay in the motor home like you did before."

She sighed. "I told you I wouldn't take your bed this time. I meant it. This is a nice hotel in a good neighborhood. There's plenty of security. I'll be fine."

He nodded grumpily. "I'll send a driver for you in the morning. Don't leave the hotel without him."

She heard the chill in her own voice when she replied a bit curtly, "I'm not a member of your team to be given orders by you, Wade. While I appreciate your concern, I prefer to make my own decisions."

He had the grace to look sheepish as he parked the car. "I was barking orders, wasn't I?"

"Yes, you were."

"Sorry. Habit, I guess. At the track, I tend to be in take-charge mode."

"With the crew, that's fine. With me, not so much."

He chuckled wryly. "Yeah, I got that. But I still don't like leaving you here."

"I got that, too. I'll be fine, Wade."

"So you keep saying. May I at least walk you up to your room?"

She moistened her lips, wondering if that was such a good idea. She couldn't help remembering the kiss outside her parents' home last week. Thinking back to how tempting it had been to drag him off to a private place and let nature take its course. But she had come to her senses since then, she reminded herself sternly. As long as she and Wade kept their distance, there was no reason he couldn't walk her to her door like an old friend.

"If it makes you feel better," she said magnanimously.

His lips twitched in response to her tone, but he reached for his door handle without responding.

"Hold on," she said when a sudden beeping sound filled the quiet car. "Let me see if this is important before we go in."

She pulled her cell phone from the pocket on the

outside of her small bag and opened it to read the text message that had just come through. Half expecting the sender to be Davida—her mother never having quite gotten the knack of text messaging—she nearly dropped the phone when she read the ominous words displayed on the backlit screen.

Maybe she made a choked sound. Or maybe Wade picked up on the tension that suddenly gripped her. "What is it? What's wrong? Is it your mother?" he asked urgently, reaching out to grip her arm.

Wordlessly, she handed him the phone.

He read the message, then cursed fluently beneath his breath. "That settles it," he said, his voice rough and uncharacteristically harsh. "I'm not leaving you here. You're staying in the motor home tonight."

"But I—"

His hand shot up, palm toward her as he stopped her in mid-protest. "Don't argue with me this time, Lisa. I know you aren't a member of my crew and I know you don't like it when I tell you what to do, but I don't care. Either you go back to the track with me, or I stay here with you. I'm not leaving you alone after this."

She looked numbly down at the phone screen. *Think you're safe just because you ran? I will find you.*

Reading the words again sent another cold chill down her spine. She didn't know how Norris had gotten her number. Whether he really knew where she was or was making a vague threat to frighten her out into the open.

He had definitely succeeded in frightening her. There

was no way she wanted to stay in that hotel suite by herself tonight. "I'll go back with you," she muttered numbly.

Though Wade looked a bit surprised by her capitulation, he didn't press his luck. He started the car. "I'll have someone collect your bags and take them to the track."

She had no doubt that he would make that happen very efficiently. Wade was in full take-charge mode again—and for once, she was in no mood to argue with him.

LATE THAT NIGHT, Lisa lay in the bed in Wade's motor home and listened to the muted sounds coming from outside. Different track, different state than last weekend, but she suspected that eventually the campground sounds all seemed familiar no matter where the RV was parked.

She rolled over onto her other side and closed her eyes, but sleep continued to elude her. She supposed she shouldn't be particularly surprised that she was lying in his bed again. Did anyone ever win in a battle of wills with that stubborn, bossy man? Certainly none of the fifty or so people who answered to him on the team.

At least she had talked Wade out of sleeping on the couch, which seemed like a particularly bad idea tonight, when she was feeling a bit too vulnerable to have him so close by. She had finally convinced him that she would be safe in the motor home with its high tech security system and nearby neighbors.

There was nowhere safer for her to be than in the restricted RV lot, surrounded by drivers and their families who were all well guarded from overeager fans and potential threats, she had added. Wade had reluctantly agreed and had gone off to bunk in Jake's bus again, but only after giving her a ten-minute lecture about not leaving the motor home without an escort or walking around the track this weekend without making sure someone was with her.

So here she was again. In Wade's bed. Alone. And unhappily aware that she wished he were here with her.

JAKE DID NOT QUALIFY as well as everyone had hoped, ending up in the eighteenth starting position. Considering the way he complained about the car's handling, he insisted that he was lucky to have finished that high. Ronnie took the pole, to his wife and crew's delight.

As happy as she was for Ronnie, Lisa could see the tension that gripped Jake's crew. Jake had declared the car "junk" and was pessimistic about their chances of getting it fine-tuned in time for the race, especially since there were certain changes they were forbidden to make between qualifying and starting the race, itself. The only way he could switch to the backup car was if he crashed the qualifying car in practice, which he certainly wasn't allowed to do intentionally, and even then, he would have to start from the very back of the field.

Although Wade kept reassuring Jake that the crew would soon have the car performing well—reminding him that they'd certainly done so last week—Lisa could tell that it was different this time. Last week the changes had been relatively minor—wedge and air pressure adjustments, a little pit stop tweaking. This time it was going to take more work.

Wade stayed busy all day Friday and when she saw him, he was terse and distracted. Not rude, but definitely concentrating on his job. Because she respected that and because she knew it was difficult for him to do so when he was undoubtedly worried about her, she stayed out of his way. She watched from the periphery for a while, then worked quietly for a few hours in the motor home, calling no attention to herself. He looked in on her occasionally to make sure she was safe and had everything she needed, but the attention felt rather perfunctory, as if she were just another item on his checklist of responsibilities.

Because Wade and the crew were going to be busy until late Friday night, she told him not to worry about her for dinner. She had plenty of food in the RV, she assured him, and there was a program on television she wanted to see that evening, anyway. While that wasn't exactly true, she figured she could find something to hold her attention for a few hours.

Reassured that she would be spending the evening safely ensconced in his motor home, Wade seemed to put her out of his mind even before they parted. Propped against the pillows of his bed with a soft drink and a bowl of microwave popcorn a couple of hours later, she flipped channels idly on the plasma screen until she found an action movie that she liked.

She'd seen this film a couple of times, but it could always be counted on to make her chuckle. And besides, the lead actor was hot. She needed whatever distraction she could find to keep her from thinking about that creepy text message, even though she had convinced herself that Norris—or whoever had sent it—didn't really have a clue where she was. However he had found her number, she was in no danger from him now.

At least, that was what she chose to believe.

Because she didn't need to pay attention to what little plot there was to the movie she'd selected, she opened a book to read while the sound of the television kept her company. She was just starting to nod off when Wade buzzed the intercom from outside and brought her quickly to her feet. She was decently dressed in drawstring waist, navy plaid cotton pants and a loose navy T-shirt, so she didn't bother with a robe or shoes when she opened the door to him.

"I know it's getting late," he said. "I saw the lights were still on, so I thought you were still awake."

"I was just watching TV," she assured him, moving out of the doorway and motioning him inside. "Do you need some of your things?"

Though he closed the door behind him, he remained just inside the motor home, looking poised to leave at any moment. "I just wanted to make sure you're okay before I turn in for the night. Is there anything you need? Did you have dinner?"

He looked so tired, she thought, studying the lines around his eyes and mouth. Almost dispirited. Were things really looking this grim for the upcoming race? And did it really matter too horribly if they were? Jake was sitting pretty solidly in the top ten. One less-than-stellar finish wouldn't knock him out of The Chase, would it?

She knew even as the thought occurred to her that Wade wouldn't be satisfied with that line of reasoning. He approached every race with the same intense determination to win. There were no "good-enoughs" in his vocabulary. Just win or lose. And anything other than first place was a loss at the back of his mind.

But was that the only thing bothering him this weekend? Or did genuine concern for her have something to do with the grim look in his eyes?

"I had a can of soup and some popcorn for dinner," she told him, still searching his expression closely. "A nice, lazy evening. How did your meetings go?"

He shrugged. "We'll see how things work out in practice tomorrow."

"I was glad Ronnie did so well in practice. Katie said he really wants a win since he hasn't had one in quite a while."

"Yeah, that would be great for Ronnie."

"But you still want Jake to win."

He gave her a tired smile. "Of course."

"Did you ever get dinner?"

"I, er, had something. I think."

If he couldn't even remember, it meant it had been too long since he'd eaten. And whatever he'd had must not have been particularly filling.

"Sit down," she said, motioning toward the built-in booth table. "I'll make you a sandwich before you head for Jake's motor home."

"You don't have to do that."

"Wade." She planted her fists on her hips and gave him a look. "You're almost swaying on your feet. I'm sleeping in your bed tonight. The least I can do is make you a sandwich."

She hadn't meant to say it quite that way, of course. The brooding look in his eyes intensified when she referred to sleeping in his bed, but he let it go, merely nodding. "All right, that sounds good. Thanks."

As he slid into the booth Lisa opened the refrigerator door. The driver Wade employed kept the motor home well stocked with Wade's favorite foods. Without even asking, she took out mustard rather than mayonnaise, cheddar cheese rather than American, bread-and-butter pickles rather than dill. She stacked the ingredients onto slices of whole wheat bread, added a handful of sour-cream-and-onion chips on the side and slid the plate in front of him.

He had watched her closely while she'd prepared the meal. "I see you haven't forgotten what I like."

"I remember how you like your sandwiches," she replied casually, turning back to the stove to take the steaming teakettle off a burner. "Would you like some herbal tea? It'll help you relax."

"I'd rather have a cola."

She poured him a cup of tea. "You don't need the caffeine this late. Drink the tea."

His mouth quirked at one corner. It wasn't exactly a smile, but close enough to give her a little satisfaction. "Getting back at me for being bossy last night?"

"Maybe. What are you going to do about it?"

He chuckled and reached for his cup. "I guess I'll drink the tea."

Sliding onto the bench across from him, she held her cup loosely between her hands. She could almost see some of the tension seeping from him and it felt good to know she could take credit for that. To keep him distracted, she chatted lightly while he ate, telling him an amusing story about a particularly stupid criminal she had once prosecuted and how frustrated the defense attorney had become simply trying to keep his client from self-destructing in court.

Wade didn't say much, but she could tell she had his attention. When she'd finished that anecdote, he asked a question that led to another, so that they passed nearly a half hour without mentioning racing or Jesse Norris.

Which didn't mean, Lisa mused, that he didn't think about the sport. She was well aware that no matter how much attention he seemed to be paying to her, part of his mind was still fully focused on getting Jake's car across the finish line in first place.

It would always be this way. With Wade—as with her dad, and so many others obsessed with this demanding career—racing came first.

Vaguely depressed then, she set her empty teacup down. "Do you want something else? I've got cookies in the cupboard—or rather, *you* have cookies in the cupboard."

Smiling a little, he shook his head. "I'm good."

"You haven't finished your tea."

"It's cold now."

"Let me heat it up for you...."

He reached across the table to catch her wrist as she started to slide out of the booth. "I'm fine, Lees."

She froze in response to his touch. "Um...yeah. Okay."

She thought he would release her then, but he continued to hold her hand in a light clasp. His thumb moved slowly against the inside of her wrist and she wondered if he felt the way her pulse hammered there. Probably. As hard as her heart was beating suddenly, how could he miss it?

"Thanks for the sandwich," he murmured. "I guess I was hungrier than I realized."

Looking down at his tanned, work-roughed hand covering her lighter, softer one, she cleared her throat silently before answering. "My pleasure. You're sure there's nothing else you need?"

In response to the silence that followed her question, she lifted her gaze slowly to his face. The way he was looking back at her made her heart leap straight into her throat. And the answer to her question hung heavily between them—obvious, but unspoken.

He slid out of the booth, drawing her with him as he rose to his feet. She stood in front of him, looking upward, trembling a little as she sensed his intention. When his head lowered, she lifted her face to meet him. Her hands slid up his chest as he gathered her closer and then her arms were around his neck as she allowed herself to be swept into his kiss.

His left hand tangled in the back of her hair, Wade

tilted her head to a new angle, allowing him to deepen the kiss. She felt the slightest tremble course through him and into her as she nestled into his arms.

There had been electricity between them before, but it felt different somehow this time. Maybe it was because it had been so long since they had been together, or maybe maturity had added a new complexity to the attraction between them. Or maybe it was the awareness of the high stakes involved this time, at least on her part. Because she wasn't at all sure she could walk away so easily this time.

He broke the kiss, but kept his hand in her hair, his mouth very close to hers, so that she felt his breath warm against her damp lips when he murmured, "I'd better go."

"It's too late," she said, her voice husky. "Stay here."

"I don't think that's a very good idea."

"I'll sleep on the couch."

His expression was rueful when he looked down at her. "I don't think that would work."

She looked up at him steadily. "Then stay—and I *won't* sleep on the couch."

For almost six years she had lived cautiously. Protecting her scarred heart. Letting few people get close to her, playing things safe. Running from danger, both physical and emotional. Keeping Wade, especially, at a distance so she wouldn't be hurt again. Now she found herself willing to take a chance—if only to find out if there was still enough between them to make it worth the gamble.

Wade lifted a hand to her cheek, his gaze focused on

her mouth. "Remember last week, when I took a risk on a two-tire pit stop?"

Though the question confused her, as it seemed to have little to do with their current situation, she nodded against his palm. "I remember."

"Some people have asked if that decision worried me. If I was afraid that the choice I'd made might have cost us too much."

She bit her lower lip, waiting for him to get to the point.

He smoothed her mouth with the ball of his thumb, as if erasing the faint teeth marks. "I wasn't scared then," he murmured. "It was a calculated risk, and I knew the consequences wouldn't be too severe if it didn't pay off. We still had a shot at a decent finish. We weren't going to fall out of The Chase."

His mouth twisted into an attempt at a smile that didn't quite come off. "I wish I had some of that courage now," he confessed.

Had the supremely confident, utterly unshakable "Ice" McClellan just admitted that he was uncertain about what to do? That he might even be a little afraid of making the wrong move? And why did she find his admission of insecurity so darned irresistible?

She rose on her tiptoes to brush her lips across his. "Let's just call this another calculated risk," she whispered and then pressed her mouth more firmly against his.

Wade murmured something that might have been agreement, but she didn't ask him to repeat it to be sure.

CHAPTER ELEVEN

LISA STIRRED AGAINST THE PILLOWS the next morning, feeling full consciousness slip into her mind and shoo away the remnants of sleep. She tried for a moment to cling to a particularly nice dream, but it was too late. Fully awake now, she opened her eyes.

She was alone in the bed, though the pillow next to hers bore a head-shaped dent. She smiled. The window blinds were closed, so that only the thinnest slivers of sunlight were visible, but a glance at the clock let her know that it was after 8:00 a.m. Later than she usually slept. She had been pleasantly exhausted by the time she'd finally fallen asleep.

After a quick shower, she dressed in a white polo shirt and jeans with sneakers. Casual and cool for hanging around the track. Sleeveless shirts and open-toed shoes weren't allowed in the garage area, so she had dressed in a manner that was suitable for wherever she wanted to go that day. She slipped her lanyard around her neck, making sure her track credentials were clearly visible before she left the motor home.

Her steps had an extra spring to them as she walked to the garages. Fans were beginning to arrive for the events scheduled that day, so she kept her guard up as she made the short trek, but she felt perfectly safe here. Chicago and Jesse Norris seemed very far away. She felt so good, actually, that it was hard to imagine she had any problems, at all.

A very dangerous feeling, she cautioned herself. If she wasn't careful, she was going to end up in serious trouble. And she wasn't thinking about Jesse Norris at all now.

As she approached the transporter for the Number 82 car, she spotted Wade huddled under the awning with several members of the crew. Wade held a clipboard and looked extremely serious as he talked. Everyone else listened intently, bodies poised to take action the moment he stopped giving instructions.

She felt her throat tighten in response to seeing him like this. In his element. In charge. Looking so different from the man who had moaned her name last night.

Hovering nearby, she watched as he completed his impromptu meeting and sent everyone scurrying. Only then did he look at her, and she realized that he had known she was there all along. Not much slipped past him here.

Moving closer, he gave her a nod of greeting. "There are snacks inside. I think I saw Katie over by Ronnie's hauler. You can either watch practice from here or go hang out with her. Just let me know where you'll be during the day."

No "good morning." No "sorry I didn't get to stay and wake up with you." No offer to let her stay close to him and learn more about his job. Just a list of terse instructions given in much the same tone he had just used with his crew.

She tried not to take offense, though the smile she gave him felt strained. "I'll manage to entertain myself. And I'll be careful, so you don't have to worry about me today."

"I'd still like to know where you go," he said, already looking down at his clipboard.

She wondered if she was one of the items listed there for him to monitor. She hadn't really expected flowers and flattery this morning, she thought, making an effort not to pout, but a smile would have been nice.

"Lisa." He looked up at her then, frowning because she hadn't yet answered to his satisfaction.

"I'll keep you informed," she conceded grudgingly.

He nodded. "I've got to go into the garage to check on a few things before practice starts."

"Don't let me keep you."

Her irritation must have gotten through to him that time. He hesitated, and looked at her for a moment as if there was something he wanted to say, but then he merely nodded again.

"I'll see you around," he said, and turned toward the garage area, striding away from the hauler without glancing back.

"And a nice day to you, too, *Ice,*" she muttered acerbically.

Behind her, Katie giggled. "That didn't sound particularly friendly," she commented, following Lisa's gaze to watch Wade disappear into the garage. "Is Wade being a jerk this morning?"

"As a matter of fact, he is."

Katie heaved a long-suffering sigh. "It's that male chromosome. It's broken, I swear."

"Tell me about it."

"Why don't you tell me about it," Katie countered. "If you want a sympathetic ear, that is. Someone with the nice, sane female chromosome."

It was sorely tempting to tell Katie everything that had ever happened between herself and Wade, including last night. Maybe Katie could help her decide if there was any cause for optimism—or if Lisa had been destined to lose this race from the start.

"You want to go find some coffee?" Lisa asked, glancing around. "Somewhere away from these testosterone-soaked haulers?"

"As a matter of fact, I came over here to ask if you wanted to go do some shopping with Andrea and me. There's a really cool outlet mall that's just, like, a half hour or so from here. I have a rental car and a charge card and I'm ready to shop."

Andrea was newly engaged to Woodrow Racing driver Mike Overstreet, and had become a good friend of Katie's. Andrea hadn't been able to attend the race in Pennsylvania, but Katie had told Lisa all about her, promising that she would like her.

"Come on, Lisa. A girl's day out. The perfect antidote for PMS—Petulant Male Syndrome."

Lisa laughed. "You know what? That sounds like exactly what I need. I would love to go. Just let me get a message to Wade about where I'll be."

Looking around, she spotted J.R. coming out of the hauler. "J.R., would you mind telling Wade that I'm going shopping with Katie and Andrea? Tell him I don't know when I'll be back but I've got my cell phone with me."

Though he looked distracted, J.R. nodded. "I'll tell him. Have fun."

Lisa tossed her head. "I intend to."

PRACTICE WASN'T QUITE a disaster, but it wasn't what Wade would have called a success, either. Jake was still unhappy with the car's handling and his lap times confirmed that something wasn't right. If they didn't figure out what was wrong and get it fixed during the race, Wade figured they would be lucky to finish on the lead lap.

Hungry, tired and frustrated, he took a break for lunch during the middle of the afternoon. Despite his concentration on his work, he'd been bothered all morning by the way he'd parted with Lisa earlier, so he took advantage of his brief downtime to go looking for her. He didn't plan to offer an apology, exactly—after all, it wasn't as if he'd snapped at her or anything—but maybe he should remind her that he wasn't at his best, socially, when he was working.

As far as talking about what had happened between them last night and what it meant for the future, well, he couldn't even think about that yet, much less discuss it. Not if he intended to get through the rest of this working weekend with any semblance of concentration.

She wasn't in the hauler. He asked Digger if he'd seen Katie or Lisa, but Digger merely shook his head, adding that Ronnie was taking a nap in his motor home, resting up after practice. Since that told him Lisa wasn't hanging out there, Wade figured she had to be in his motor home.

He didn't get worried until he found his motor home empty.

He tried calling her cell phone, but all he got was her voice mail. He left a rather terse message for her to please call him immediately, but his phone didn't ring as he prowled around the track compound, looking everywhere he could think of for her.

"Hey, Ice." Vince skidded to a halt in front of him. "Chuck wants to talk to you. He thinks he's got a couple of new ideas about those adjustments we need to make, wants to run 'em past you."

"Okay, yeah. Tell him I'll be there in a few minutes. You haven't seen Lisa, have you?"

"Lisa?" Vince shook his head. "Not since this morning."

"How about Katie Short?"

"Nope. But about Chuck—"

"I'll be right there, okay?" Wade repeated impatiently. "Just give me a few more minutes."

"All right. Jeez, no need to get all testy." Still muttering, Vince stormed off.

Wade flipped his cell phone open again and dialed Lisa's number. His teeth clenched when he heard her prerecorded message again. "Damn it, Lisa, *call me!*"

SHOPPING WITH Katie and Andrea was a pleasant experience. Lisa had a very nice time, spending entirely too much money at the outlet mall. Katie couldn't resist purchasing several adorable little girls' outfits, even though she was barely showing in her pregnancy, and Andrea purchased a few cute tops for herself.

Breathtakingly beautiful, with long blond hair, a stunning face and a truly spectacular figure, Andrea Kennedy was surprisingly down-to-earth and likeable, which was probably why she and Katie had become such good friends. While she was obviously accustomed to male attention, Andrea was still getting used to being engaged to a man who lived in the racing world fishbowl.

It felt good, she said, to spend a few hours away from the whirlwind with two other women who understood what it was like to feel as though she were being constantly watched and evaluated. Still, Lisa could tell that Andrea found her new position exciting, that for the most part she enjoyed the attention.

Both Katie and Andrea seemed happy with their lives in the shadows of their famous partners, she mused as she carried her bags into Wade's motor home. Andrea had expressed no interest in a career of her own, and Katie was content with tutoring during the school year and anticipating being a mother. They knew what was expected of them, understood the delicate balance of sacrifices and rewards. And they were satisfied with the choices they had made.

As happy as she was for them, Lisa felt an odd emptiness deep inside her after the excursion.

She had just walked into the motor home when someone loomed out at her. "Where have you been?"

Gasping, she staggered backward, dropping packages all around her feet. "Wade! You scared the daylights out of me."

"That's because you didn't bother to check the security system to see if anyone was in here."

She winced. "I guess I was thinking about something else."

"And is that your excuse for not telling me where you were going—even though I specifically asked you to keep me informed of your whereabouts?"

"You didn't ask me anything," she countered defensively. "You ordered me. But I left a message with J.R. about where I would be. He said he would tell you."

Wade frowned. "J.R.?"

She nodded. "Didn't he tell you?"

"He said something earlier this morning about you being with Katie. He didn't say you would be leaving the track. I just assumed he meant you were at Katie's hauler. Or her motor home. But when I couldn't find you at either of those places—"

"I told him we were going shopping. And I said you could call my cell phone if you needed me."

"I tried calling your phone. Several times. You didn't answer."

Now it was her turn to frown. "You did? I don't remember hearing it ring."

She pulled her phone out of its holder on her belt and grimaced when she saw the symbol that told her she had voice mail messages. A couple of button presses told her what had happened.

"Sorry. I set it to silent when I cleared that message last night, and I forgot to change it back this morning, so it didn't ring when you called. I never thought to check for messages, since I wasn't expecting any calls. And to be honest, I didn't want to read any more threatening messages from Norris while I was having such a good time with my new friends."

"A lot of good it did you to have your phone with you."

Sighing with mounting impatience at his attitude, she reached down to retrieve her dropped bags and toss them on the table. "Look, I'm sorry you didn't understand the message I left for you and that I missed your calls. But all I did was go shopping with Katie and Andrea. You never said I was forbidden to leave the track."

"I didn't think I'd *have* to say it," he snapped. "The whole point of you being here is to take advantage of the security here at the track. Beyond the gates there's no one watching out for you. If Norris had followed you here, you'd have made yourself a sitting duck on a shopping excursion. Not only that, but you'd have endangered Katie and Andrea at the same time."

Planting her fists on her hips, Lisa faced him defiantly. "Okay, that's enough already. We went shopping. I was careful. Katie knows the whole story so she was as alert as I was to any potential problems. There weren't any."

"Great. And while you were shopping and ignoring your phone, I was going crazy here. How am I supposed to concentrate on my work when I have to worry about what you're up to?"

"I'm so sorry I interfered with your all-important job!" she snapped, finally losing her temper. "Maybe I should have just sat quietly in a corner of the hauler until you had time to throw me a scrap of attention. Is that what you want from me, Wade?"

"I never said—" He stopped and drew a sharp breath, pushing his hand through his hair.

"This is ridiculous," he said after a moment, his own temper now firmly back under control. "I don't expect you to sit in a corner, Lisa. And you're right, you don't need my permission to leave the track. I appreciate that you tried to leave word for me, though J.R. isn't the most reliable messenger around. I just think it would be best if you stay close for the rest of the weekend, especially since there are going to be over two hundred thousand spectators here tomorrow. Maybe that message last night didn't worry you, but it scared the hell out of me."

She nodded stiffly. "I wasn't planning to leave the track again this weekend. And, yes, it scared me, too. But I told the Chicago police about it and forwarded them the message and there doesn't seem to be anything more I can do about it. I just…I just needed to get away from it all for a little while, you know?"

He looked at her moodily for a moment, then nodded and changed the subject. "So, you want to go have some dinner? Bubba and Tony are frying catfish and hush puppies back at the hauler. A special request from Jake and Ronnie."

Lisa wasn't as good as Wade at pulling herself back together after their skirmish. As tempting as it was to stay in the motor home and seethe about what she had perceived as an unfair attack, that would be petty. She lifted her chin. "Sounds good. I'll just put my things away and then I'll be along."

"I'll wait and walk you over."

"That won't be necessary. I'd like to freshen up for a few minutes, and I'd hate for you to have to wait for me."

"Lees—"

She turned away deliberately from his partially outstretched hand. "I'll see you at the hauler, Wade."

It might have been more dramatic if there had been room in the motor home for her to stalk past him and close the bedroom door behind her. As it was, he pretty well blocked the aisle. She moved to one side, looking pointedly at the door. Pretty nervy of her to kick him out of his own motor home, but he was the one who had started this quarrel.

He didn't linger to argue longer. He merely dropped his hand and walked past her, quietly letting himself out.

"SO, YOU WANT TO TELL ME what's going on between you and Wade? Did you have a fight?"

Sitting in a lawn chair next to Katie, Lisa balanced a paper plate of fried fish filets, hush puppies and cole-slaw on her knees and pretended to be hungry. She shrugged in response to Katie's low-voiced question. "Is it that obvious?"

"Not from looking at him, of course. Wade never gives anything away. But you've been looking ready to kick something ever since you joined us for dinner. Since I know you were in a good mood after we went shopping, and since Wade mentioned that he'd seen you at his motor home, I put two and two together."

Wade never gives anything away. That was an understatement. He'd made it clear enough that he'd been annoyed with her for leaving without making sure he knew about it, but even in his anger he'd been fully under control. She'd been on the verge of throwing things, but he'd just packed it all down and asked her if she wanted catfish. And she prided herself on being so cool and collected in her work!

"He was irritated because I left the track. J.R. didn't get the message to him clearly enough and apparently Wade was worried that someone had made off with me."

"Well, that's sort of nice, isn't it? That he was worried about you, I mean."

"He was annoyed because it interfered with his work," Lisa muttered. "I didn't follow his instructions and so he couldn't mark me off his checklist."

"Oh, Lisa, surely he didn't mean it like that. He must have been frantic about you if he didn't know where you were. When he said he couldn't concentrate on his job, I'm sure it was more of a measure of how worried he was than a complaint about the inconvenience."

"I'm not so sure. The job is everything to him, Katie.

Always has been, always will be. He's never pretended otherwise."

Not even that morning, after she had made it painfully clear to him that her feelings for him had never really gone away. That she had been willing to try again if he could help her find a reason to believe they could make it work this time. She hadn't said it in so many words, but he had to have known last night had meant a great deal to her. That there had been nothing casual about it, at least as far as she was concerned.

Wade, on the other hand, had been "business as usual" from the time he'd slipped out that morning. There had been no warmth in his eyes when he had seen her again, no tenderness in his voice when he had spoken to her. If last night had meant anything to him other than a pleasant way to pass a couple of hours, or a brief stroll down memory lane, he certainly hadn't let her see it. And it hurt.

Maybe she could have competed with the job. If it had only been the job. And if she'd known for certain that she meant as least as much to him as racing did. But she hadn't been able to settle for second place six years ago, and she wasn't willing to do so now. She'd spent the first part of her life trying to get her father's attention; she wasn't going to spend the rest of it trying to hold Wade's.

"The job is important to Ronnie, too, you know. All he can think about during the season is the next race. The next win."

Lisa shook her head and smiled a bit sadly at her new

friend. "You know better than that. Yes, racing is very important to Ronnie, but if he had to make a choice, he would choose you and the baby. He would never be entirely happy if he couldn't race, but he'd make it work somehow. Because he loves you. Because he's made a commitment to you and Olivia. Don't tell me you aren't aware of that."

Katie started to speak, and then she gave a rueful little shrug. "I guess you're right. I'd hate to think he would ever have to make that choice, and I will certainly never willingly put him into a situation where he would have to pick—but I know he would choose his wife and child. Unlike some of the other drivers I know," she added with a frown.

Glancing across the pavement to where Wade sat with Ronnie, Jake and Digger, Lisa mentally added his name to that list.

"I'm sorry, Lisa. I was hoping things would work out between you and Wade, you know? I've come to think of you as a good friend over the last couple of weeks."

Looking determinedly away from Wade, Lisa forced a smile. "I feel the same way about you. And that doesn't have to end just because I'm not going to be hanging around the tracks with Wade. Have you forgotten my father owns the team? I can visit the tracks any time I want to, with or without Wade's approval. I feel more a part of this team now and I'm going to make sure Dad lets me stay involved, even if only peripherally."

Katie looked as if it hadn't really occurred to her just how Lisa was connected except through Wade.

"Oh, my gosh. I'd almost forgotten…I mean, this whole operation will probably belong to you someday, won't it?"

Exactly what her mother had implied. And as she had then, Lisa demurred, "Someday, far in the future, maybe…"

"So in an indirect way, you're sort of Wade's boss, aren't you? He's got some nerve yelling at you for not following his orders."

"I'm not Wade's boss in *any* way," Lisa corrected her quickly. "This company is my father's, not mine. Not for a long time, if ever."

"At least you don't have to worry about Wade romancing you in an attempt to take over the business," Katie said tactlessly.

Lisa winced. Now she *would* have to consider that possibility, even though she found it hard to believe. For one thing, Wade hadn't exactly romanced her. So if that was his agenda, he wasn't particularly good at it.

She politely declined an invitation to join the weekly Bunko game, telling Katie she was tired. Katie didn't look as though she bought the excuse, but she didn't argue, sensing that Lisa wasn't in the mood for a party.

She didn't even wait for Wade to walk her back to the motor home after dinner. Instead, she fell into step beside Jake as he headed back to his own coach, where he would relax and then turn in early, as was apparently his practice on the night before a race. She knew Wade watched them leave the hauler, but he didn't try to follow.

"Man, that was some good fish, wasn't it?" Jake

asked, rubbing his tummy in satisfaction. "Bubba sure knows how to cook a catfish."

"It was delicious. It's hard to find catfish and hush puppies cooked just right in Chicago."

"I'll bet. Rumor has it that you're thinking about coming back to North Carolina."

She shrugged. "Probably. I'd like to live closer to my parents."

"I don't blame you. They're great people. Woody's an old tyrant, of course, but he's more bark than bite. And your mother is one of the nicest ladies I've ever met."

Pleased, she smiled at him. "She likes you, too. She told me you send her flowers for every holiday. She loves flowers."

"My pleasure. Here we are at your door, safe and sound."

She turned to him at the bottom of the steps. "Thank you for the escort. And I hope you have another great race tomorrow."

"Thanks." A shadow of concern passed through his dark eyes, but he didn't let his smile dim. "I'd love a win here. Every one of us wants at least one chance to kiss those bricks."

"You'll have that chance," she predicted confidently. She didn't know that he would win tomorrow, but Jake was too good a driver not to be on top eventually. Everyone seemed to accept that a championship was inevitable for him. It was just a matter of when. And she had a feeling the time was now.

"Knock wood when you say that," he said, taking her

hand and rapping it against the side of his own head a couple of times.

She laughed. "Superstitious, are you?"

"Sugar, we all are. If I win tomorrow, you'll have to come knock me in the head before every race."

"I don't think I can guarantee that."

"If it were up to Wade, you could."

Her smile faded. "Yes, well…good night, Jake."

He touched her arm. "He's a great guy, you know. The best friend I've ever had. But he's a total wipeout when it comes to expressing his feelings. Which doesn't mean he doesn't have any."

"Jake." She patted his hand. "I'm glad Wade has such a good friend. I hope the two of you stay pals forever and win a dozen championships together."

"But you want me to butt out, right?"

"Right."

He squeezed her fingers, then stepped back. "You got it. Good night, Lisa. Sleep well."

"You, too." She turned and walked inside the motor home, knowing that Jake waited until she was safely inside before walking away.

LISA FOUND THE HORSESHOE by accident that night. Stumbling around in the bedroom, still completely distracted by Wade's odd behavior, she opened the wrong drawer, thinking it was the one Wade had emptied out for her things. Instead, she found herself looking down at a neatly folded stack of white T-shirts and a cheap metal paperweight tucked into one corner.

Moving very slowly, she reached out to pick it up, holding it in the palm of her hand as she stared at it. Shaped like a horseshoe with the head of a proud-looking horse in the center, the lightweight trinket was obviously inexpensive, pretty much useless for its intended purpose. The formerly shiny silver paint had begun to flake, exposing areas of dull gray beneath. The green felt backing had worn off in places, revealing the hollow inside.

It might well have been a time machine, so quickly did the sight of it carry her back to a night more than six years earlier.

She and Wade had been at a carnival. He hadn't been overly enthusiastic about going, but when she'd seen the bright lights and spinning Ferris wheel, she had talked him into it. Because he had always indulged her while they were dating, it hadn't been hard to convince him.

They had walked hand-in-hand along the midway, eating cotton candy and watching people on the rides and at the so-obviously-skewed games of "chance." Wade had thrown a baseball at a stack of wooden milk bottles and had won her a purple teddy bear, which still sat in a corner of the closet in her bedroom at her parents' house. She'd been amused by the way he'd strutted a little when they'd walked away from the booth—so typically and endearingly male.

She had been so in love with him that night that she'd been almost giddy with it, almost able to completely ignore the doubts that had already set in about their relationship. The diamond ring on her left hand had seemed almost like a promise that night, rather than the ominous symbol it had begun to feel like.

She'd won the horseshoe trinket from a quarter-a-play claw machine on her third attempt. Delighted when it dropped into the slot, she plucked it out and turned victoriously to Wade, who stood nearby self-consciously holding the purple teddy bear.

"For you," she had said, holding it out to him with exaggerated ceremony. "For luck at the racetrack next weekend."

He'd had a funny look on his face when he accepted the gift. "Uh, thanks," he'd mumbled, tucking the horse-shoe into his pocket. "But unlike a lot of superstitious guys in racing, I don't really believe in luck. I believe in hard work and perseverance."

The prosaic comment had dimmed some of the giddy pleasure she'd been feeling that evening. As they left the carnival a short while later, she had wondered if he would ever even look at the prize again, or if he would simply toss it in the trash when he got home.

A week later, she had broken off their engagement.

And yet, here it was. Obviously something Wade carried with him from track to track. The flaking paint and worn-off felt could only be attributed to a great deal of handling over the years. From the pattern of wear, she could almost see him holding it, absently rubbing his thumb over the smooth surface.

With the wisdom of maturity—and having come to know Wade a bit better during the past couple of weeks—she wondered now if Wade had been touched by her gesture and was characteristically unable to express his emotions with anything other than his usual gruff logic. Had he hung on to the souvenir just for luck, despite his denial of superstition, or did it have a deeper meaning for him?

Would Wade ever be able to open up enough to her to tell her exactly how he felt about her—or about anything other than racing?

CHAPTER TWELVE

SUNDAY WAS THE USUAL hectic pandemonium, beginning before dawn and going hard all morning. The sheer number of people at this enormous facility was mind-boggling. The excitement, the energy, the adrenaline, it was all almost overwhelming.

Lisa stayed close to the team, sitting in on the church service and the drivers' meeting, hanging around the hauler, watching as Jake and Wade worked the media and the fans. Wade acknowledged her presence, asking occasionally if she needed anything, but she stayed out of his way, calling no extra attention to herself.

An hour before the race was supposed to start, she grew a little restless, weary of trying so hard to remain quiet and invisible. Thinking of Davida, she wandered toward the souvenir trucks. Her friend would love a few trinkets from this famous track.

Truckloads of T-shirts, hats, jackets and other officially licensed memorabilia were available at every race. Woodrow Racing sent out several trucks every week packed to capacity with assorted merchandise bearing the faces of Jake, Ronnie, Mike and Scott. Thousands of items changed hands even as she walked through the

rows, eager fans perfectly willing to part with their
money in exchange for a souvenir to show their dedication to their favorite drivers.

It seemed that almost all the fans wore their alle-
giance on their clothing. Driver images, sponsor logos,
car numbers—few seemed to be neutral. Lisa felt a bit
conspicuous in her plain yellow T-shirt and jeans. Oddly enough, she didn't even own a shirt with a driver's
picture on it. She thought it would feel strange to have
Jake's face, handsome as it was, emblazoned across
her chest.

Two young women, perhaps in their late teens, un-
deniably sisters, passed her on the crowded pathway.
They wore Scott Rivers T-shirts and baseballs caps and
clutched glossy hero cards bearing the young driver's
image, biography and racing statistics in their hands.

"Can you believe we got his autograph?" one of them
said with a sigh.

"I know. He was like two feet from us. And he was
so hot!"

"Even better than on TV. And that smile…"

Their gusty sighs lingered behind them as they
walked on, disappearing into the crowd.

Lisa shook her head with a smile. Scott was twenty-
two years old, still struggling with the remnants of
teenage acne, barely out of braces. He had a great deal
of promise as an up-and-coming driver, showing an impressive maturity on the track, but the last time she had
seen him in person he'd been playing with a remote
control dune buggy in the garage, running it under

everyone's feet and laughing like a bratty middle school kid. Hard for her to think of him as a "hero."

The August heat was stifling, but it didn't seem to be having much effect on the good moods of the fans who were killing time before the start of the race. Most had dressed—or underdressed—for the weather, and a majority wore a hat of some sort against the relentless sun.

Deciding that was a pretty good idea since her face was already starting to tingle despite the sunscreen she'd donned that morning, Lisa bought a purple-and-silver Jake Hinson baseball cap. She didn't put it on yet, but she would as soon as she moved out of the souvenir area. And yes, she probably could have found a cap for free back in the hauler, but it was kind of fun to shop at the track along with the other fans.

She was standing at one of the back tents, perusing a stack of T-shirts bearing the official race logo, when someone grabbed her arm in a tight grip.

She gasped and tried to jerk away, prepared to scream for help if necessary. Fear turned to surprise, which turned to anger when she realized that it was Wade holding her arm, his expression grim beneath his sponsor cap and aviator-style sunglasses.

"Wade! You scared me half to death. Are you trying to give me a heart attack this weekend?"

"I'm trying to remind you that you're putting yourself at risk every time you wander out of the restricted areas of the track," he answered her grimly. "I've been looking everywhere for you. Arnie told me he'd seen you wander off this way. You were completely oblivious to anyone around you just now. I was able to walk right up and grab your arm without you even noticing that I was nearby."

She sighed. "It's precisely because I'm surrounded by people that I feel safe enough here. Who would try anything with thousands of witnesses around like this?"

"Now you're just being naive."

"Don't you have things you should be doing?"

"Hundreds of things. I certainly don't have time to be chasing you all over the track."

"Then why are you? I can watch out for myself."

"Oh, yeah. You've done such a great job of that so far."

She shook her head in exasperation at his confrontational attitude. "Why are you acting this way?"

"Because I don't want anything to happen to you!" he snapped. "Because some psycho wants to hurt you and it's driving me crazy that you're so cavalier about that. Because you mean entirely too much to me—and I don't know how to deal with that and still do my job today."

Stunned into silence, Lisa stared up at him. Only then did she become aware of all the people around them, some of them having come to a stop to gape openly at them. Someone lifted a camera and took a picture of crew chief "Ice" McClellan having a very public—and uncharacteristically emotional—spat with a woman.

Her cheeks went hot. Wade's turned suspiciously dark beneath his glasses. She saw his chagrin at having lost control even that briefly.

"I've got to get back to work," he muttered, tugging

the brim of his cap lower over his face. "Could you at least stay by the hauler during the race?"

She nodded.

Wade turned on one heel, waiting only for her to fall into step beside him before heading back to the hauler so quickly it was all she could do to keep up with him. She didn't protest. It was going to be a while before she could find her voice again.

HAVING BEEN THE OBJECT of too much attention already, Lisa stayed in the hauler during most of the race, watching televised coverage. The announcers kept up a lively commentary, speculating about Jake's chances of pulling off back-to-back wins, talking about how well Woodrow Racing had performed during the season so far, giving kudos to Woody as owner and the drivers and crew chiefs for the outstanding jobs they had done. Especially Wade, whose gutsy calls and intense focus made him one of the most respected crew chiefs currently in the business.

They alluded to that single-minded focus after a reporter tried to stick a mic into Wade's face during the early part of the race and got a string of monosyllabic responses to her perky questions. "Doesn't look like he's in the mood to talk," one of the announcers said with a chuckle.

"Nope. He's concentrating on getting the Number 82 car back into Victory Lane," his cohort said cheerfully. "Uh-oh, looks like trouble in Turn Three."

The cameras panned to a car spinning on the track

while the others swerved frantically to avoid him. Not a Woodrow car, Lisa noted automatically, though her attention was only marginally on the race. She kept thinking about the words Wade had said to her earlier.

Because you mean entirely too much to me—and I don't know how to deal with that and still do my job today.

It was as close as he had come yet to telling her he still had feelings for her. Strong feelings, if the expression on his usually inscrutable face had been any indication. And he had acknowledged that those feelings, in addition to his concern for her safety, were making it hard for him to concentrate on his work. Something else she had never expected him to admit.

She stared blankly at the screen, aware that people came in and out of the hauler during the race, some of them looking at her oddly, but acknowledging them with no more than distant nods.

You mean entirely too much to me. It wasn't exactly a declaration of love, but from Wade, was it possible that it meant the same thing? And if it did, well, then what? Even if she loved him, too—and that was a question she couldn't examine too closely just then since she suspected she already knew the answer—what did that mean for either of them?

"I'm telling you, folks, this guy wants a win." One of the announcers hooted, and Lisa turned her attention back to the screen. She straightened on the black leather couch, watching as Jake steadily advanced through the pack, passing one car after another with an almost reckless ferocity that made the announcers marvel at his sheer determination.

"He's putting it all out there," one of them said. "He's not playing it safe and just trying to stay in the points chase."

One of the others laughed. "Jake Hinson doesn't know how to play it safe. It's all or nothing for that guy. You can bet his crew chief is telling him to calm down, be patient, keep the big picture in mind."

Wishing she had accepted the headphones someone had offered her earlier, Lisa jumped to her feet. Everyone else was outside now, watching the conclusion of the race. She wanted to be with the rest of the team.

Her Jake Hinson cap in place, she hovered at the edge of the pit, watching with the pit crew. Tension gripped all of them, their body language indicating that each one of them was mentally urging Jake on.

Someone slipped a set of headphones on over her cap. Looking around gratefully, she smiled at J.R., then listened to the chatter in her ears.

The spotter shouting instructions, "Clear low, clear low, *go!*"

Jake shouting back, "Where's Ronnie? Has he got my back?"

And then Wade, calm, reassuring, "You're doing great, Jake. Stay cool. Stay clean. You can do this."

No one could have possibly known from listening to that smooth, composed voice that Wade had recently had a near-meltdown of his own, Lisa marveled. He was a little too good at tamping down his emotions when he had to. Better than she was, obviously, she thought, glancing up at him as he sat high on the pit box, the undisputed leader of this team.

He wanted this win. The hunger was written in every line of his lean, taut body. Maybe he could hide all his other emotions, but he couldn't hide that. This was when Wade was happiest, the most fulfilled. This was what guided his every waking moment, she mused thoughtfully. He wanted this win. And the win after that. He wanted the championship. And another after that.

Wade was a racer, as was her father, and Jake and all the crew members surrounding her in their purple and silver uniforms and all the crews in the other pits, equally invested in their drivers' performance on the track. It was a culture of its own, and few outsiders would ever fully understand it. As for herself—well, she felt as though she existed somewhere in the middle, not fully belonging to either the racing or the non-racing world.

Maybe that was because she had never really committed to either option.

With Ronnie on his back bumper, Jake sped around the third place car. And then dropped low and took the lead. The crew erupted into cheers. J.R. grabbed Lisa and spun her around, setting her back on her feet laughing and breathless. He shouted something to her, but there was entirely too much noise for her to hear anything except the voices in her headset.

The last lap had everyone in the stands on their feet. Jake and Ronnie battled for the lead—teammates and friends, but still competitors, both of them wanting to be the first to cross that finish line. They crossed it almost side-by-side, though Jake had just enough lead to make it official. He had won his second race in two weeks. And the hardworking, dedicated crew that had played a huge part in getting him there went wild in celebration.

Jake was able to show off this time, spinning circles and burning his tires so that a huge cloud of acrid smoke enveloped the car and then drifted into the stands. His jackman and tire carriers performed a happy dance in the pit that ended with them in a heap on the ground, slapping each other's helmets and generally making fools of themselves. Other crew members leapt nimbly over them as they dashed toward Victory Lane.

Wade climbed down from the pit box, a look of quiet satisfaction on his face. He spotted her standing there and he went still, reaching up slowly to remove his headset. She couldn't see his eyes behind his dark glasses, but she knew they were locked with hers. And she was afraid that her eyes were all too revealing as she moved toward him.

"Congratulations," she said when she got close enough for him to hear her over the din.

"Thanks."

"I guess you'd better go join your driver. He's got some bricks to kiss, doesn't he?"

"Yeah. You'll be here?"

She nodded toward the hauler. "I'll be here."

He started to move away. Aware of the eyes watching them, Lisa reached out to catch his sleeve. "Wade."

He looked down at her again. "Yeah?"

Getting up on her tiptoes, she brushed her lips across his. It was an apology, of sorts, for worrying him earlier. A reiteration, in a way, that she really was happy for his win. That she knew how much it meant to him.

Wade swept her into his arms, kissing her with an intensity that curled her toes in her sneakers. If brains could do burnouts, there would be smoke coming out of her ears, she thought dazedly, her arms around his neck.

He released her as abruptly as he'd grabbed her, lingering only long enough to make sure she was steady on her feet before bolting away to celebrate with his team.

"Wow." The reporter who had tried unsuccessfully to draw Wade into a conversation earlier stood nearby, a look of astonishment on her carefully madeup face. She held her microphone at her side while her cameraman stood behind her, camera perched on his broad shoulder. "Who'd have thought Ice McClellan could kiss like that?"

Quickly recovering her professionalism, she tilted her head questioningly at Lisa. "Mind if I ask who you are?"

Lisa was already walking toward the hauler, with J.R. moving to get between her and the intrusive camera. "Just a friend," she said over her shoulder.

She figured it was as good a description as any. For now.

LISA GOT A CALL WHILE SHE was waiting in the hauler for Wade to finish with his post-win responsibilities. Seeing Davida's number on the screen, she took the call.

"Great race, wasn't it?" Davida asked cheerfully. "Two wins in two weeks. You must be a good-luck charm for the team."

A couple of crew members had mentioned something like that when she'd come back into the hauler. One had gone as far as to half-seriously suggest that she should never miss another race.

Because she had no interest in serving as anyone's good-luck charm, Lisa said simply, "The crew did an amazing job getting the car in great shape and Jake did a fantastic job driving it to the front."

"Spoken like a true representative of the team," Davida teased. "Anyway, congratulations on the Woodrow Racing first and second finish. Now I have some good news for you from here."

Lisa sat up straighter on the couch. "What news?"

"Jesse Norris was recaptured this morning. He's back behind bars, under heavy security. He's being charged with several counts of assault and attempted murder, among other things. He won't be bothering you again."

Feeling relief flood through her, Lisa murmured, "That *is* good news."

"No kidding. After that scary message you received, you must feel like celebrating to know he's back in custody. I know the atmosphere in the office is going to be a lot more relaxed tomorrow. I just talked to Joe Engler, by the way. He's making a fast recovery and hopes to be back at work in a few weeks."

"I'm glad to hear that, too."

"So, anyway, even though I'm sure you'll want to take the rest of your vacation, it must be good to know that you can come back any time you want to, right?"

"Um, yeah. Right."

"I'll let you go. I know you're still at the track and you're probably really busy. I just couldn't wait to tell you the news. I wanted to be the first," she admitted.

"Thanks, Davida. You really took a load off my mind." And now Wade could relax about her safety, she thought as she disconnected the call. There was no need for her to even travel with the team to the next race.

She sank back into the couch cushions, trying to decide exactly how she felt about that.

"YOU'VE BEEN AWFULLY quiet this evening," Wade commented, glancing away from the road ahead long enough to study what he could see of Lisa's expression in the darkened car. "Tired?"

"A little."

He would have thought she would be in a better mood tonight. Jake had won the race and Jesse Norris was back behind bars. While he figured the latter was a great deal more important to her than the former, she had seemed pleased earlier by Jake's win.

As for himself, there was no question. As happy as he was about the win, he was much more satisfied with the knowledge that the jerk who had tried to hurt Lisa wouldn't be seeing daylight again for a very, very long time.

And yet...

"So," he said, looking intently forward as he guided the car toward her parents' neighborhood. "Are you going to tell your folks about Norris now?"

"Maybe. I haven't really decided."

"You know, we'll be in New York this next weekend. A road race. Totally different from the two races you've seen so far. Jake doesn't have a prayer of winning it, but I think you'd find it interesting."

She gave a little laugh. "What makes you think he can't win?"

"Experience. Jake always struggles on the road courses. If he finishes in the top ten we'll be happy."

"Then, I hope he does."

"Yeah. Me, too. So…you want to go? If you don't want to stay in the motor home, you could always use your dad's suite—now that you don't have to worry about Norris showing up."

"I'll…I'll think about it, okay?"

He tightened his hands around the steering wheel. This was even more awkward than he had expected. Their first private conversation since he'd blurted that stupid, public admission that he cared about her.

He still couldn't believe he'd said those things. Not like that, anyway. He'd still been trying to come to terms, himself, with his feelings for her. He hadn't been ready to discuss them with her. Certainly not in the middle of a race crowd less than an hour before the green flag fell.

Maybe he'd been hoping that she would pretend he'd never said it. Or that she would have written it off to the heat of the moment. Or maybe he'd hoped that she would say something similar back to him. She hadn't.

She hadn't said much at all to him since they'd left Indiana, other than to inform him that Norris had been recaptured.

He wished he was better with words. Yeah, sure, he knew how to talk to the media, how to lead his team, how to calm his driver. But when it came to finding out if Lisa was going to leave him again, he didn't even know where to begin.

He stopped at the gate of the Woodrow estate and keyed in the security code. The massive gates slid smoothly open, allowing him to drive through.

"It looks like my parents have already turned in," Lisa commented, glancing at the few lighted windows in the house.

"I won't come in, then."

She nodded, and he got the impression that she was not disappointed. Maybe she just needed to think about everything that had happened between them that weekend. He could certainly understand if that was the case, since he'd been doing a lot of that, himself.

He turned to face her after turning off the engine. "We should probably talk about what happened between us this weekend."

He watched her throat work with a hard swallow. "I suppose we should," she agreed, sounding as reluctant as he felt to get into that sticky area.

"But not now, of course."

"No," she agreed with almost comical haste. "Not now."

"I'll call you sometime tomorrow, okay? Maybe we can have dinner or something before it's time to leave for New York."

"Maybe."

Not exactly a commitment. But then, she'd always been leery of commitments when it came to him, he thought ruefully.

He reached for his door handle.

"You don't have to walk me to the door."

Ignoring her protest, he climbed out of the car and walked around the front to open her door. Carrying her bags, he escorted her to the door, remembering the last time they had stood there. When she had initiated a kiss that had shaken him to his boots, leaving him thinking there was the slightest chance that he could have the future he'd once planned for them, after all.

It was when he'd woken up beside her in his motor home and had realized how very right it had felt to do so that he'd panicked. He'd asked himself what the heck he thought he was doing setting himself up to be hurt and disappointed by her again. Knowing as he did that nothing had really changed between them.

So he'd bolted, straight back to the one place where he'd always felt at home and in control. The track.

He could tell by her body language that there would be no kiss tonight. He didn't know whether she'd had second thoughts about spending the night with him, or if she was annoyed with him for pulling away from her afterward. Not to mention yelling at her in front of a few thousand people. He wouldn't blame her, either way.

"We'll talk later," he said.

She nodded and keyed in the security code to her parents' house. "Good night, Wade."

He set her bags just inside the door, then backed away. "Good night, Lees."

She started to close the door between them, then pulled it open again. "Wade?"

He paused on the top step, turning quickly. "Yeah?"

"Thank you again. For everything. You've been a very good friend."

Friend. He mulled the word over a moment, trying to decide how he felt about it. Before he could make up his mind, she closed the door.

CHAPTER THIRTEEN

LISA'S APARTMENT IN Chicago felt musty, almost unfamiliar, even though it had been only two weeks since she'd left it. She had wandered through it aimlessly Tuesday afternoon, trying to avoid looking at the bedroom window where someone—presumably Jesse Norris—had tried to break in. Norris was safely in custody again, so she didn't have to worry about him, but she still thought she might move to another apartment complex soon. One with more security.

She sat now at her kitchen table with a cup of coffee and her laptop, trying to catch up on some of the things she'd missed at work during the past two weeks. It was harder than usual to pay attention. She was battling too many emotions to put them easily aside so that she could concentrate on her work.

Guilt was probably the most prominent of those emotions. She had left Charlotte that morning without even telling Wade goodbye.

Her father had tried to talk her out of going, reminding her that she had two weeks left of her vacation. He'd asked if she'd had a fight with Wade.

"No, Wade and I didn't have a fight," she had replied

evasively. "I just need to go back to Chicago sooner than I had expected. For, um, work reasons."

He hadn't believed her, and neither had her mother, though her mom hadn't tried to change her mind. "Do what you need to do, sweetheart," she had said. "But know that our doors are always open when you want to come home."

Promising to be back soon, Lisa had boarded a plane, feeling like a coward as she had run away from North Carolina. From Wade.

She couldn't think straight when he was in the room with her. Not even in the same state with her, apparently. She had needed the distance between them in order to separate what her head was telling her from the messages that came from her heart.

She had told her parents to let Wade know that she'd gone back to Chicago to take care of some personal business, and that he could call her cell phone if he wanted to talk.

He'd probably gotten that message by now. He hadn't called. She didn't think that he would.

She had hurt him six years ago. She didn't know why she could see that now when she couldn't then. Maybe it had been finding that little horseshoe trinket tucked away with his T-shirts. Maybe it was just that she'd been able to see more of the real Wade this time than she had when girlish infatuation and unrealistic hopes had clouded her vision.

Leaving like this, without even a goodbye, had probably hurt him again. After all he had done for her, he hadn't deserved that. She had regretted her decision halfway back to Chicago, but by then it had been too late to change her mind.

She thought about calling him. She actually picked up the telephone and dialed the first three digits of his cell phone number before hitting the disconnect button. And then she hid her face in her hands and wondered how she had ended up in this condition after taking such pride in her competence and decisiveness for so long.

WADE TOLD HIMSELF IT WAS NICE to have his motor home back. Heck of a lot more convenient than schlepping back and forth from the track to a hotel room or camping out on Jake's couch. His own toiletries in the bathroom, his clothes in his own closet, his favorite foods in the kitchen. His own bed.

With no one in it but himself.

Some people were meant to share their lives. Some had the talent to be able to compartmentalize their time between career and family. Some were lucky enough to find mates who understood their obsessions and found a way to work around them. Ronnie and Mike came immediately to his mind. And then there were those, such as Digger and himself, who were better off single, concentrating on the careers that consumed their every waking moment.

At least he had managed to avoid Digger's mistakes, Wade told himself as he sat on the end of the bed in his motor home, staring morosely at the TV that wasn't turned on. Digger had been through several divorces before coming to the same realization that Wade had finally accepted a few days earlier. When he'd found out that Lisa had gone back to Chicago. Without even telling him that she was leaving.

He took pride in knowing he'd given nothing away when Woody told him. He'd merely lifted an eyebrow, nodded and gone back to work. He would be willing to bet no one could tell that inside he felt as though he'd just crashed full speed into a wall.

Wasn't that how he'd earned his nickname?

So here he was. Alone on a Thursday night before qualifying. At a road racetrack that would offer exactly what he and Jake thrived on—a challenge. The car was in good shape, Jake was pumped and ready to qualify. It was going to be a great weekend, win or lose.

He stood and opened his T-shirt drawer, taking out the old paperweight. It was looking pretty bad, most of the paint flaked off, the felt worn off the bottom. It was probably made of lead or something and was poisoning his Tees. He should probably throw it away.

For several long moments, he stood there, looking down at the worthless trinket in his hand. And then he put it back where it had been and slowly closed the drawer.

"PITIFUL. JUST PITIFUL."

Lisa looked up Saturday morning from her cluttered desk to the woman standing in her office doorway. "What?"

Davida entered the office and moved a stack of paperwork out of a chair so she could sit down. "You could be watching race practice in New York but instead you're here on a Saturday working. You had two more weeks of your vacation left and what do you do? You come back to work. On a weekend. Pitiful."

Wrinkling her nose, Lisa demanded, "Aren't *you* here on a Saturday?"

"Well, yeah. But I didn't have anything better to do," Davida replied with a shrug. "Might as well wade through some paperwork rather than sit at home and watch dust collect on the furniture."

Lisa knew that Davida was going through a spell of empty nest syndrome. Divorced, she had raised a son on her own. Her son had recently moved out to go to college on the west coast. Now Davida stayed busy with work and her passion for racing and football—in that order. She said it was enough to satisfy her, but Lisa couldn't help wondering if that were really true.

They talked a few minutes about the two races Lisa had seen. She shared a few behind-the-scenes anecdotes that made Davida happy. Davida asked questions about some of her favorite drivers and Lisa answered what she could. "You have to remember," she added, "I was sort of lying low during both races. I didn't hide, exactly, but I stayed close to Dad's teams."

"That just had to be so cool," Davida said with a wistful sigh. "All those racing people. All that excitement. Especially since your driver won both races."

"Yes, it was very exciting," Lisa murmured, though she wasn't thinking about the races. "But it was time for me to get back to my real life. My own work."

"It's good to have you here," her friend said, standing. "Even though I still think it's pitiful that you'd run back to work the minute the coast was clear."

Lisa laughed and waved Davida away. Her smile faded the moment she was alone again.

Davida had no way of knowing, of course, that Lisa hadn't been running toward her work as much as she had been running away from Wade. And she felt more like a coward now than she had when she left Chicago for North Carolina.

BUBBA AND TONY served barbecued chicken, grilled corn on the cob and deli-style potato salad Saturday. The food was good, or at least, Wade assumed it was from the way everyone was raving about it. As for himself, he ate without really tasting, his thoughts far away.

Jake was talking to his publicist about the next day's schedule, while Digger and Ronnie were huddled in a discussion about race strategy and the other members of the crews perched in various locations to eat and talk. Ninety percent of those conversations probably revolved around racing in some way, Wade figured. Like himself, a lot of these guys didn't really know how to talk about anything else.

"How's your chicken, Wade?" Katie asked, wandering over to stand next to his chair after finishing her own meal.

He had been so deep in his thoughts that it took him a moment to process what she had asked. "Um…it's good, thanks. Did you get enough to eat?"

"More than enough," she said with a smile, patting her tummy. It seemed to be true that there was a special glow about an expectant mother.

Because he rarely conversed with Katie alone, he searched awkwardly for something to say. "So, how are you feeling?"

"Great. I miss Lisa this weekend, though."

So did he. But instead of saying so, all he did was nod.

"Will she be back for another race this season, do you think?"

He stared down at his plate. "I don't know."

"Have you asked her?"

"I asked her to this one. She went back to Chicago, instead."

Maybe his tone had given away too much. Katie perched on the edge of an empty lawn chair next to him and studied him somberly. "She's really into you, you know."

He wasn't sure what she meant by that. Especially since Lisa had gone back to Chicago rather than come with him to the track.

"I have a feeling you're still into her, too. Though I wonder if you've ever admitted it. Even to yourself."

He leveled a look at Katie, getting a blandly innocent smile in return. "You can't yell at a pregnant lady," she informed him. "Even one who's giving you unwanted advice about your love life."

"Yeah? Watch me."

Not in the least intimidated, she giggled and patted his arm. "Okay, I'll butt out. Just let me say one more thing?"

He nodded reluctantly.

"As obvious as it is to me that you two are perfect for each other, I can't help but wonder if either of you have ever talked about your feelings. I mean, you aren't exactly the chatty type, and I don't think it's much easier for Lisa to open herself up. And yet, you're both such nice people. Despite your nickname, I don't think you're at all coldhearted, Wade. Just very guarded. But maybe there are some things that are worth taking a risk for?"

She stood without giving him a chance to respond—not that he knew what he would have said. Patting his shoulder like the kindergarten teacher she was, she said, "Okay, I'm shutting up now, and I promise I won't bring it up again. I just really like you both, you know? And I can't help thinking that you could work things out between you—if you would only really talk with each other."

More touched than he might have expected, Wade nodded. "Thanks, Katie," he said, his voice gruff. And he left it at that, because he couldn't think of anything to add.

LISA WAS STILL AT THE OFFICE when Wade called her Saturday evening. It was just after six in Chicago, an hour later where he was, but she would have thought he'd still be huddled in a meeting with his crew about the next day's race. She certainly hadn't expected him to call her.

"Is this a bad time?" he asked, sounding a bit awkward.

"No. I'm at my office, just wrapping up to go home."

"Working late on a Saturday?"

"I have a lot of catching up to do."

"Yeah…well…" His voice trailed off.

"Wade?" She gripped the phone more tightly. "Is there a reason you called?"

"You left without saying goodbye."

She winced in response to the accusatory undertone in his otherwise uninflected words. "I know. I'm sorry. I just…needed to come back to work."

"You had two more weeks of vacation left."

"Have you ever taken *your* full vacation time?" She knew the answer to that, of course. Her mother had told her that Wade rarely used all the time he accrued as a longtime employee of Woodrow Racing.

He left the question unanswered, choosing instead to say quietly, "I miss you here, Lees."

Such a simple, unvarnished statement. And yet it absolutely floored her. From Wade, that was practically a flowery monologue.

"I miss you, too," she whispered honestly. "But—"

How could she explain that being there for him wasn't enough for her? That she wished she could be more like Katie and Andrea and so many of the other women she'd met, for whom racing was almost as much their passion as it was for the men they loved. Women who reveled in supporting their partners' careers and raising their children and finding fulfillment in family and charity work. She felt almost petty and self-absorbed for not being more like them, and she resented that feeling because she knew it wasn't fair to compare herself to them.

Typical of Wade not to let her take the easy way out. "But what?"

"But I need my work," she said finally. "Just as you need yours."

After a lengthy, taut pause, Wade demanded, "Have I ever once asked you to give up your work? Or even implied that it's any less important than my own?"

She was surprised by the sudden irritation in his voice. "I, um—"

He cut into her stammering to say coolly, "If you're going to write us off, Lisa, at least base your decision on reality, not what you think I want or don't want."

"How can I know what you want or don't want," she was stung into retorting, "when you've never told me? You never tell me *anything* that you're thinking or feeling."

"I'm not the only one, apparently. This is the first I've heard that I haven't been supportive of your career."

She started to argue, but then realized that he'd made a legitimate point.

"I know I'm not very good at communicating, but I'm not the one who keeps leaving without explaining why," he added, just in case she hadn't caught on.

"No," she murmured after several long moments. "I guess you aren't."

"Look, we need to talk. Really talk, for the first time ever, I guess. But not like this. Not on the phone."

Just the thought of that long-overdue discussion made her heart thump with apprehension, making her wonder now just which one of them had been the most fearful about sharing feelings. But because she was ready to finally stop being a coward, she said, "Yes, we do need to talk."

"I'll call you after I get home from the race, okay? We'll work something out."

"All right. Good luck tomorrow, Wade. I really do hope Jake does well."

His voice softened just a little. "Thanks, Lees. Take care of yourself, okay?"

"You, too."

She disconnected without saying goodbye.

Maybe the reason she kept doing that was because she wasn't sure she could ever really say goodbye to Wade, she mused as she gazed somberly at the phone in her unsteady hand.

STILL DISTRACTED BY THAT PHONE CALL, still trying to reason out exactly what Wade had meant by the things he had said and what they would say when they finally had that talk he'd mentioned, Lisa stepped off the elevator in her apartment building and turned toward her door. Often, she walked up the four flights of stairs to her apartment for the exercise, but tonight she was just too tired and too emotionally drained to expend the effort.

It was only a little before 8:00 p.m., and the building was quiet. Most of her neighbors were other singles, many of whom were out on a nice summer Saturday evening. Pushing a hand through her hair, she wondered without much interest what she had in her freezer to prepare for dinner—

Someone jumped out from behind the stairwell door.

Lisa jerked out of the way at the very last moment,

barely avoiding a violent collision with a tall brunette in a dark shirt and jeans.

Before Lisa could completely regain her balance, the other women rushed toward her again. Only then did Lisa see the knife in the woman's hand.

CHAPTER FOURTEEN

IT WAS PURE instinct that made Lisa leap sideways again. Perhaps, it was the basic self-defense training her father had insisted she take before moving so far away from home, but she ducked just in time. The tip of the sharp blade raked the sleeve of her favorite gray-and-white striped blouse, catching for a moment in the soft fabric and leaving a long, jagged tear behind.

For just a heartbeat, Lisa wasn't sure if she'd been cut along with her shirt, but she didn't take time to assess her condition. Nor did she try to be a hero and fight back. The first rule of every self-defense course was simply to get away and out of danger.

She bolted down the long hallway, yelling for help, with the knife-wielding woman pursuing her, furiously screaming words Lisa didn't completely take in. Mostly they seemed to be threats and curses.

To her intense relief, someone was at home, after all. A door opened at the end of the hallway and the tenant stepped out curiously.

"Hey!" The burly young man in a gray Northwestern T-shirt, a neighbor Lisa had seen around but had never actually met, didn't hesitate to come to her aid when he saw what was happening.

"Call the cops!" he shouted to someone still inside his apartment, and then threw himself at Lisa's attacker.

The woman with the knife was young, but sturdily built. Taller than Lisa, and perhaps twenty pounds heavier. Still, she was no match for this athletic young man, who dove beneath the flailing knife blade and took her down in a classic football tackle.

Now that reinforcements had arrived, Lisa turned to help, kicking the knife away from the cursing, struggling woman's hand before she could do any damage to Lisa's rescuer. She made no effort to temper the kick; if she broke a few of the woman's fingers, she didn't really care.

Another woman approached them then, looking apprehensively from Lisa to the couple struggling on the carpeted hallway floor. The young man sat on top of the bucking brunette, holding her arms splayed beside her head, his face red from the effort. "Did you call the police?" he asked breathlessly.

The newcomer, a petite, attractive Asian with a look of horror on her youthful face, nodded. "They're on their way."

The brunette erupted in a whole new string of curses, doing her best to get away from the man and go after Lisa again. "If you don't stay still, I swear I'm going to knock your head off," he finally shouted at her in exasperation, his strong Southern accent denoting him as a non-native. And obviously someone who would gladly follow through on the threat if given any further provocation.

The woman finally stopped struggling, though she continued to glare at Lisa with a look that contained so much hatred that Lisa shuddered. She recognized her attacker now.

"You're Jesse Norris's girlfriend," she said, staring down at the rage-twisted face. "I saw you in court."

"You took him away from me," the woman shrieked, her red-rimmed eyes leaking furious tears. "You made the jury believe all your lies and they sent him away!"

"They weren't lies and you know that." Lisa looked at the young couple who had come to her aid, figuring they deserved an explanation. "I'm a criminal prosecutor. Her boyfriend is a thug who deserves to stay behind bars for a very long time."

Nodding in comprehension, the young couple both looked at the attacker again, their expressions making it clear they were on Lisa's side. Norris's girlfriend spat out another curse at Lisa and then turned her head to one side, the fight draining out of her as she accepted her defeat.

THREE POLICE OFFICERS arrived moments later, two of them taking Norris's girlfriend into custody and another remaining behind to take statements from Lisa and her neighbors.

More spectators had gathered by that time, and Lisa was resigned to seeing a report in the news before it was all over. Her neighbor—whose name, she knew now, was James Holland—seemed to revel in the attention, enjoying seeing himself in the role of hero. Because she was so grateful to him, Lisa played along, assuring anyone who asked that she would have been in grave danger if it hadn't been for James and his girlfriend, Cai.

"I really want to give you something in appreciation," she assured him when some of the uproar had died down. "You took a risk getting involved like that when so many people would have locked their doors and played it safe."

"Not where I come from they don't," he said with a shake of his sandy head. "When our neighbors are in trouble, we help 'em out. And we don't take payment for doing so," he added proudly.

"Where *are* you from?"

"Tuscaloosa, Mississippi, ma'am. You're not originally from Chicago, either, are you?"

She shook her head. "North Carolina."

He grinned appealingly. "I thought so. You can't ever really lose all that Southern accent, can you?"

"I quit trying a long time ago," she admitted.

"Me, too. I figured it was a lost cause in my case."

They chatted a few minutes longer, Lisa learning that he was a second-year law student with ambitions of returning home to open his own law office. Cai was also in law school. Both adamantly insisted that they had only been doing their civic duty to come to Lisa's aid, and both refused any mention of reward for doing so.

"Are you a NASCAR fan, by any chance?" Lisa finally thought to ask James.

"Are you kidding? I've been following NASCAR

since I was just a little bitty thing. I guess you are, too, being from North Carolina and all?"

She smiled. "It's a little more than that. My father is Woody Woodrow. Have you heard of him?"

He looked thunderstruck. "Your dad owns Wood-row Racing? Man, that's my favorite team of all time. Jake Hinson, Ronnie Short, Mike Overstreet and that new kid, uh—"

"Scott Rivers."

"Yeah, Rivers. Gonna be a driver to reckon with when he gets a little more experience under his belt."

"I think so, too. So will you at least let me send you and Cai to a race? My treat. They'll be back in Michigan next weekend, which isn't so far to travel, and I'm sure my father would be able to arrange tickets and garage passes and accommodations for you, if you're interested. Or if you can't go next weekend, maybe some other race?"

James looked dazed. "Garage passes? For the Michigan race? Oh, man."

She smiled. "Does that mean you are interested?"

"Are you kidding? I'd just about give my left—er, arm for that. You're sure it wouldn't be too much trouble for you?"

Shaking her head, she assured him, "Once my father finds out what you did for me, he'll want to name a holiday after you. I'll set everything up and get back to you soon, okay?"

She had no doubt that her father would go out of his way to make the arrangements after she told him that

James had saved her from serious injury, at the least. And she would have to tell him, she thought as she locked the door to her apartment a short while later. She intended to call him immediately, before someone else heard about the incident and said something to him about it. There was already a message on her answering machine from a *Tribune* reporter, wanting details about the attack.

Drawing a deep breath to steady herself, she sat on her couch and dialed her parents' number. "Virginia? Hi, it's me. Is my father available?... Daddy, there's something I need to tell you. And don't overreact, okay? Because I'm fine, really."

AFTER A VERY RESTLESS NIGHT, Lisa was still sleeping when her telephone rang at 9:00 a.m. on Sunday. She answered groggily, thinking it was probably someone from her office. Her phone had rung off the hook until well after midnight, as word had spread among her friends and associates about what had happened to her.

"H'lo?"

"Why the hell didn't you call me?"

She blinked and sat upright in the bed. "Wade?"

"You didn't think I would want to know that someone tried to kill you after we spoke last night? I had to find out from your father this morning?"

"I didn't want to upset you. I knew you needed to concentrate on the race today. Darn it, I told Daddy not to tell you until after the race."

"Would you forget the race?" he asked, his voice

rising. "Do you really think that matters when you've been attacked? Are you all right?"

He continued to prove that he could surprise her. "I'm fine," she said quietly, subdued by his tone. He had definitely been shaken by hearing this news—more so than she would have expected.

She was beginning to believe that Wade really did care very deeply about her. And that he had his own way of expressing his feelings that spoke as clearly as romantic speeches from some other men.

She gave him a quick summary of the incident, downplaying how close the woman had come to putting the knife into her, telling him about the heroism of her idealistic young neighbor.

"Daddy's making arrangements to give him the VIP treatment at the track next weekend," she added. "You'll probably have a chance to meet him."

"I'd like to meet him," Wade agreed. "He and his girl-friend are welcome to watch the race from the pit, if they want. Heck, after what he did for you, I'd almost let him call the race."

"Speaking of which," she added pointedly, "aren't there things you should be doing there? The pre-race stuff is probably already underway, isn't it?"

"Yeah." She hadn't expected to hear the reluctance in his voice. After a brief hesitation, he added, "You know I would come there today if I could. But I can't, Lees. There are too many people depending on me here."

Just the fact that he'd felt the need to explain meant a great deal to her. "I wouldn't expect you to neglect your responsibilities there. And as I assured my parents last night, I don't need anyone to come here and hold my hand. I'm fine. Both Norris and his crazy girlfriend are behind bars, and there's no reason for me to be afraid. The apartment management is already looking into increasing security to prevent future problems like this, which I heartily endorse, but I feel completely safe now."

"You were incredibly lucky to survive a knife attack without an injury."

"Yes, I was," she agreed heartily. "I didn't try to fight her. I just ran, yelling for help. I'm so grateful that James was around to hear me."

"Sometimes running is the best way to protect yourself."

She bit her lip and then murmured, "Yeah. Sometimes."

She heard him say something to someone else and heard other voices calling his name in the background. "You should get back to work," she told him. "Don't let the team down because of me."

"You're sure you're all right?"

"I'm sure. Go call your race, Wade. Get Jake up to the front, okay? I'll be watching on TV."

"I'll give you a wave. But I'm still ticked off that you didn't call last night, by the way."

"You can yell at me again later. When you aren't so busy."

"Count on it. I've got to go now."

"All right. 'Bye, Wade."

"'Bye, Lisa. I, uh—I love you, you know."

He hung up before she could respond.

She didn't realize she was crying until a tear dropped onto her lap a few moments later. Mopping at her wet cheeks with one hand, she set the telephone in its cradle, her shaking hands making the task more difficult than it should have been.

It hadn't been the most romantic declaration in history. But it had still made her heart swell to near bursting. She knew how very hard it must have been for Wade to say.

He had told her he loved her before, back when he had asked her to marry him. But the words had been practiced then, almost perfunctory—something expected along with the presentation of a ring. She hadn't been completely convinced then that he meant them. She was now.

She loved him, too. Maybe even more now than she had back then, when her judgment had been clouded by unrealistic longings.

Which didn't mean, she thought, drying her eyes and sliding out of the bed, that their future together was guaranteed. As Wade had said, they needed to talk.

WADE'S PREDICTION PROVED to be correct. Jake didn't win the race. He wasn't even in the top ten. He struggled throughout the event, almost spinning out a couple of times.

Considering everything, Lisa supposed Jake's sixteenth place finish was satisfactory. Since several of the other points leaders also struggled during the road race, he didn't take a big hit in points standing, so he was still sitting pretty for the final ten races.

As the cars ran the final laps, the camera panned at one point to Wade who, seeing the lenses aimed in his direction, gave a faint smile and a wave. The announcers remarked at how unusual it was for him to do either one during a race.

"He must be in an exceptionally good mood this afternoon," one of them commented.

"Probably thanking the fans for all the support Jake Hinson has received this season," the other commentator suggested. "You gotta admit, it's been a great year for the Number 82 crew."

Even though Lisa knew that Wade was indeed grateful to all the fans, she knew exactly who Wade had acknowledged. He had promised to wave to her. And he had. Because he had wanted her to know he hadn't forgotten about her, even while he gave his full concentration to his job, she thought, getting all misty again.

Thanks to an amazing pit stop during a very late caution, Ronnie crossed the finish line first. Sitting alone in her living room, Lisa cheered, knowing how thrilled Ronnie and Katie and Digger and all of the Woodrow Racing team would be. Ronnie's pit crew would certainly be congratulated for their speed and efficiency during the entire race, especially that vital final stop.

The announcers were certainly making a big deal of the third victory for Woodrow Racing in as many weeks. Things couldn't look better for her dad's team, she thought with a smile, knowing how happy he must be right now, despite his and his wife's health problems.

This was what he had been working for so very long. And because it meant so much to him, her mom would be happy, too.

Her private celebration of the team's good fortune was short-lived. She spent the rest of the evening thinking about Wade—and trying to decide exactly how far she was willing to go to try to make a future with him in a sport that demanded everything of its participants.

EVEN AT JUST AFTER NOON on a Monday, the sprawling Charlotte, North Carolina airport was bustling. Passing the gift shops and food court without even being tempted to linger, Lisa headed straight for the rental car counter where a car was reserved for her.

No one waited to meet her, since she hadn't told anyone she was coming. She didn't have to stop by baggage claim, since she had packed everything she needed in a carry-on to save time.

It wasn't like her to act on sheer impulse, but she had certainly done so this morning when she'd called her boss on the way to the airport and told him that she was taking the remainder of her leave. He'd obviously thought that she needed time to recover from her ordeal with Norris's girlfriend, and she hadn't bothered to change his mind, though it made her seem a bit wimpy. She couldn't be bothered to fret about that right now.

She needed to talk to Wade. And she couldn't wait any longer. Besides, this was the day she was most likely to be able to get him to herself for a few hours, the day after a race, before he was too heavily involved in preparations for the next one.

Strapped behind the wheel of the compact sedan she had rented, she turned on the radio to keep her company during the forty-minute drive to the shop, where she was sure she'd find Wade. She needed the noise to distract her from her nerves about the wisdom of this trip.

Still, she only half listened to the music and ads blaring from the speakers. She was actually thinking about turning the radio off to let her fret and stew in silence when a news flash caught her attention.

"A tragic accident on Lake Norman earlier today has left one man dead and two critically injured," a woman's well-modulated voice reported. "NASCAR racing star Jake Hinson was boating with a friend when their boat was struck by another craft moving at high speed. Hinson's passenger, who has not been identified pending notification of relatives, was killed on impact. Hinson and the driver of the other boat have both been hospitalized. The hospital is not releasing details of their conditions at this time, other than to say that their injuries were serious. We'll get back to you as soon as we have more details. In other news—"

Lisa snapped off the radio and dug frantically for her cell phone, making an effort not to wreck her car in the process. Because she was shaking so hard, she took the next exit ramp, pulling into a service station and throwing the vehicle into Park even as she speed-dialed her parents' telephone number.

Virginia answered. "They aren't home, Lisa," she

said as soon as Lisa identified herself. "They've gone to the hospital. I don't know if you've heard, but—"

"All I know is that Jake was hurt in a boating accident and that someone...someone was killed," Lisa blurted, her heart pounding with dread. "Who was with him, Virginia? It...it wasn't Wade, was it?"

"Oh, no, honey, it wasn't Wade. I think your daddy said it was an old friend of Jake's from high school."

Lisa almost choked on a flood of tears that were a mixture of relief and sadness. "How is Jake, do you know?"

The pause that followed the question made her chest tighten again. "I don't know," Virginia said finally. "But last I heard, it wasn't good."

Forgetting for a moment that the housekeeper couldn't see her, Lisa nodded. "Okay. I'm on my way to the hospital now. Call my cell if you hear anything in the next half hour or so, will you?"

"The next half hour?" Virginia repeated quizzically. "Are you—?"

"I'm just leaving Charlotte. I'll explain later."

"You be careful. I can tell you're upset and I don't want you driving recklessly."

"I'll be careful," she promised as she ended the quick call.

She wouldn't take any risks, she vowed, starting the car again. Her parents needed her now. Wade needed her. And this time, she would be there for him, as he had been for her when she had needed him most.

CHAPTER FIFTEEN

THE WAITING ROOM WAS SO crowded that Wade felt almost as if there wasn't enough air to supply everyone. His chest felt tight as he struggled to draw in a deep breath. It wasn't a big area. Because of Jake's celebrity, the hospital had provided a private waiting room in which they could wait for word without being observed or disturbing other equally worried families who wouldn't appreciate public attention.

Wade sat alone in one corner, and even though he was surrounded by friends and coworkers, no one tried to approach him. They assumed he wanted to be left alone—and they were right.

Woody sat in a chair on the other side of the room, his walker propped beside him, his wife clinging to his hand from her chair on his other side. Ellen's face was pale, Wade noted, and he wished he could go to her and reassure her that Jake would be all right. Because he couldn't make that promise, he stayed where he was, lost in his own anguish.

Katie and Ronnie were there, Katie uncharacteristically subdued, her eyes red from crying. Ronnie hovered near her, trying to talk her into leaving the hospital and getting some rest. Wade heard him assure her that someone would call the moment there was some news of Jake's condition, but Katie wouldn't leave. Jake had no family of his own, she insisted. The Woodrow Racing family was all he had, and family stayed with their own in times of trouble.

Mike and Andrea hovered in one corner of the room, along with Scott and Digger and Bodie and Dick and a half dozen other key Woodrow employees. Even more had shown up earlier, but Woody had sent them away, saying that a general announcement would be made as soon as there was any news.

Pam paced the halls of the hospital, returning dozens of telephone calls from anxious sponsors and other racing associates, dealing with the clamoring media outside, checking in occasionally to see if there had been any updates from the medical staff. Ominously, nothing new had been reported in the past forty-five minutes.

Ellen had said something earlier about calling Lisa, but Woody had suggested they wait until they had somthing more definitive to tell her.

"No need to worry the girl unnecessarily," he'd insisted gruffly, obviously refusing to believe that everything wouldn't turn out fine. Woody Woodrow wouldn't even acknowledge the possibility of disaster, a trait that served him well in his careers, but sometimes impeded his view of reality, Wade reflected somberly.

Knowing Lisa would probably hear about the accident through news reports, he kept his cell phone clipped to his belt. He couldn't call her yet—didn't trust his voice to remain steady—but he would answer if she called him. And he would try very hard to find the calm place inside him that he relied upon when everything was going to hell on the racetrack.

He couldn't help wondering if his friend would ever rocket around a racetrack again. And even having the question cross his mind was so devastating that he slumped forward in his vinyl seat, propping his elbows on his knees and putting his face into his hands.

He didn't usually consider himself a particularly religious man, but he prayed then.

LISA SAW HIM SITTING there the moment she walked into the waiting room. He looked so alone. So despondent. It broke her heart.

She stopped for a moment by her parents' chairs, promising she would be back to explain to them how she had gotten there so quickly. They didn't try to detain her as they followed her gaze toward Wade, who was still sitting with his head in his hands. She heard a low buzz of conversation as the others in the room recognized her, but other than acknowledging Katie and Ronnie with a nod, she didn't pause on her way to Wade.

She knelt in front of his chair, placing her hands on his, so that they cupped his face. "Wade."

His head jerked up abruptly. In one smooth movement, he was on his feet and Lisa was in his arms.

"I don't know how you're here," he muttered into her ear, his voice unsteady, "but I'm glad you are."

"I was coming to see you," she whispered, clinging to him. "That talk we were going to have, remember?"

He nodded and drew back, looking suddenly aware of the attention they were getting from other parts of the room. Still, he didn't let go of her hands, clinging to them so tightly she might have winced had she not been holding onto him every bit as firmly.

"How is Jake?"

"He's in surgery. We haven't heard an update in a while. It's pretty bad, Lisa."

The stark assessment made her throat tighten. "I'm so sorry. How did it happen?"

Anger darkened Wade's eyes. "Some idiot was show-ing off, waving to some girls on the shore. He came up behind Jake's boat without even watching where he was going. Slammed right into them before they had a chance to avoid him. Both Jake and his friend, Eric, were thrown from the boat. Eric didn't make it. Jake was pinned in debris until some rescuers reached him. It's a miracle he didn't drown."

"What are his injuries?"

"I'm not sure. Broken bones, definitely. Maybe a head injury."

Which meant his racing season was most likely over, she thought fleetingly, if not his entire career. But because that was a distant secondary concern at the moment, she didn't mention it.

She drew Wade over to where her parents sat, coaxing him into joining everyone else in the vigil. He needed to understand that he was a part of this group, she decided. He'd been alone for too much of his life. It was long past time for that to change.

Her dad was becoming typically impatient and beginning to bluster threats about demanding answers from the hospital administration. Her mom did her best to calm him, but Lisa could tell that she, too, was growing anxious for news.

Wade's hand tightened on Lisa's arm when a tall, angular African-American woman in blue scrubs strode through the door of the waiting room. "That's the surgeon," he muttered, rising to his feet. "Dr. Wiley."

Lisa found herself looking for clues to Jake's condition in the surgeon's unrevealing features. Relief flooded her when Dr. Wiley smiled reassuringly.

"He's going to be fine," she announced to the room at large. "He has several weeks, perhaps a couple of months of rehabilitation ahead of him, but he should make a complete recovery. I fully expect him to be back out on the racetrack soon, regularly risking those same bones I just put back together."

Lisa almost sagged in gratitude. Because his arm had been around her shoulders in preparation for the report, she could feel the slight shudder of relief that went through Wade.

She saw that Katie and Ronnie were hugging—Katie shedding a few more tears—and that the men in the room were slapping shoulders and bumping fists, their version of celebratory hugs. Her parents were holding hands, Ellen's eyes damp, Woody's face red with suppressed emotion.

Everyone in this room cared very deeply about Jake, she realized. The man, not just the winning driver. She hoped he would recognize that, himself. Maybe it would make it easier for him to accept that there would be no championship for him this year.

Jake was going to be in recovery for a while, and then in and out of consciousness for the rest of the day while his pain was being managed, the surgeon said after wrapping up her discussion of the procedures he had undergone. After she left the waiting room, the group gathered there began to separate.

Pam went off to work on an official statement which she would personally deliver to the reporters gathered outside the hospital. Ronnie talked Katie into leaving to get some rest. She hugged everyone on her way out, lingering for just a moment to make Lisa promise that they would talk very soon.

The other two drivers and three crew chiefs drifted out shortly afterward, all of them having official duties to attend to, but all of them promising to be back to visit when Jake was up to seeing them.

And finally it was down to Lisa, her parents and Wade. The waiting room was suddenly very quiet, and felt much larger than it had only a short while earlier, Lisa thought, sinking into a chair beside her mother.

"Jake has no family at all?" she asked.

Apparently still too wired to sit, Wade prowled the room, but paused to answer her question before either of her parents could speak. "He doesn't have anyone. He was raised by a single mother who died a couple of years ago. I think he's had a couple of distant cousins pop up to claim relationship since he made it big, but he hasn't gotten close to any of them."

"How sad," she murmured. "Not to have any family."

"He has the Woodrow Racing family," her father said gruffly. "Like Katie said earlier, we take care of our own. Jake won't have to worry about being alone while he recuperates."

Lisa smiled fondly at her father, wondering why it had taken her so many years to see the soft heart inside that blustering, workaholic exterior. Maybe she'd simply needed to be away for a while. A chance to grow up and see her parents—and Wade—through the eyes of an adult rather than an indulged and sheltered girl.

She didn't regret leaving all those years ago. But maybe now it was time to come back home.

Her parents looked tired, she thought. But even as the observation crossed her mind, her dad's thoughts had already turned to business.

"We'll have to find a driver for the Number 82 car for the rest of the season, or at least until Jake's cleared to drive again," he said to Wade. "At least we can be accruing owner points for the next couple of months. You think Pete's ready to move up?"

"He's still green, but I can work with him," Wade said, leaning against the presently unoccupied reception desk. "We'll start first thing tomorrow morning, get him ready for Michigan. At least he's close to Jake's size, so the seat'll fit him. What about the Busch—?"

"Honestly, you two," Ellen said in wry exasperation,

shaking her head. "Couldn't you take a minute to appreciate that Jake's going to be okay before you start discussing his replacement for the upcoming race?"

"Racing doesn't stop because one of the drivers is hurt," Woody answered with a pragmatic shrug. "Even if the worst had happened with Jake, there'd still be a race in Michigan this weekend. That's the way it's always been. That's the only way he'd want it."

Men. Lisa shook her head before saying, "Mom's tired, Dad. You should both go home and get some rest. I'll stay around here with Jake if Wade needs to go to the shop, and I'm sure Pam will be here most of the day. Do you have someone to drive you?"

He nodded. "Walter's waiting downstairs with the car," he conceded. Walter was the driver who usually accompanied her dad to the various racetracks. Since Woody's hip replacement, he'd been driving him around locally, as well. Ellen did very little driving since her own recent health scare.

"Good. You two go on home. I promise I'll call you if there's any news. I'll be there later, after I'm sure Jake's settled in and everything's okay."

It took another fifteen minutes to get them on their way, since Woody kept thinking of new instructions to bark at Wade. But finally Wade and Lisa were alone in the room.

"Have you had anything to eat today?" she asked him, noting the drawn look of his face.

"Breakfast."

She glanced at his watch. "You should eat something. We can go down to the cafeteria. It'll be a while before Jake's out of recovery and you can see him."

"I'm not very hungry."

"Wade." She smiled at him. "Don't make me have to get rough with you."

For the first time since she had arrived, he gave her a little smile in return. Just a hint of one, but enough to satisfy her for now. "Think you're tough enough to take me on, huh?"

"I'm Woody Woodrow's daughter," she reminded him. "Bossiness is in my genes."

"Something I suppose I should keep in mind for the future."

"Most definitely."

He seemed to give it a moment's thought, then nodded. "I've always held my own with Woody. Never had any problem getting along with him. Guess I can do the same with you."

He had a knack for saying a great deal with a few completely prosaic words, she thought as she turned toward the doorway. Maybe she was just learning to read him better—but she was pretty sure Wade had just told her that he wanted a future with her.

She couldn't help thinking back to the night he had proposed to her. "I love you," he had said without embellishment, holding out the tasteful diamond ring he had chosen for her. "I think we make a great team. Will you marry me?"

She had waited a few beats before answering, perhaps hoping there would be a little more to the proposal. At least a few mushy words. When she'd realized that he'd said all he thought he needed to say, she'd accepted the proposal with a mixture of joy and secret trepidation.

That trepidation was gone now, she realized as she walked by his side toward the doorway. But the joy was back in full force.

"Lisa." A hand on her arm, he detained her just as she was reaching out to push the door open.

She looked up at him curiously. "Yes?"

His mouth twisted a little. "It's never the right time or the right place for us to have that talk, is it?"

"It will be," she promised him quietly. "We have plenty of time for that, later."

Looking pleased with her response, he pushed open the door and escorted her downstairs to the cafeteria.

LISA WAS SITTING BY Jake's bed a few hours later when he opened his eyes, squinting against the bright hospital lighting. He was hooked up to IV bags and monitors, and his face was pale and bruised against the stark white sheets.

Yet somehow, even battered and temporarily incapacitated, there was a strength about Jake Hinson that was unmistakable, she decided, studying him as he came to full consciousness.

He looked around the otherwise empty room before focusing a bit blearily on her. "Lisa?"

"Yes. How are you feeling?"

He thought about it a moment, then summed his

condition up with a succinctness that made her have to smother a laugh.

"It will get better," she assured him. "Considering everything, you were really lucky, Jake. You're expected to make a complete recovery."

He had been brought up-to-date earlier, so he already knew that his friend had been killed and that he, himself, faced a lengthy rehabilitation. She saw the shadows cross his face as those grim facts all came back to him, but he merely nodded. Just from the little she knew about him, she understood that it would be unlike him to complain or feel sorry for himself.

"Where's Wade?"

"He had to leave for a little while. He'll be back soon. Pam's still here, by the way. Last I saw she was answering a dozen or so phone calls from the media and sponsors."

He nodded. "That's Pam. Always got a phone to one ear."

"She seems very efficient."

"Frighteningly so. She's probably already lining up interviews for me as soon as I leave the hospital." He glanced at the equipment surrounding him, then asked quietly, "Who's driving the Number 82 this weekend?"

Just like Wade and her father, Lisa thought wryly. Barely conscious and still all he could think about was racing. "Someone named Pete, from what I heard."

"Yeah, that's who I thought. Wade's going to have his hands full this weekend."

"He'll miss you."

"He'll work with his driver," Jake replied with a slight shrug that reminded her again of her father. "Pete's gonna run his first major race with the best crew and the best crew chief in the sport."

"Not that you're biased or anything."

"Just being factual," he said, and obviously believed every word of it, which Lisa thought was nice.

"I'm kind of surprised to see you here," he said a moment later. "Last I knew, you were back in Chicago. And Wade's been a real bear since you left, by the way."

"I'm back," she said simply. "I was already in Charlotte when I heard about your accident. I volunteered to sit with you while the others take care of business this afternoon. Everyone was gathered here during your surgery, but we sent them all away to come back a few at a time when you're up for visitors. My parents wanted to stay, but I convinced them to go home and rest."

"Good. They don't need to be hanging around a hospital. And while I appreciate you being here, you don't have to stay, either, Lisa. I'm sure you've got better things to do. I'll be okay."

"I'd like to stay for a little while longer, if you don't mind. My parents would feel better knowing there's someone here with you."

"No, I don't mind. Actually, I…would rather not be alone right now. I just know how bored you must be sitting here."

She smiled again. "I'm not bored at all. Is there anything you need?"

His dark eyes were tormented, but he shook his head. "No, thanks. I'm good."

He looked away, focusing on the television bolted to the ceiling at the foot of his bed, even though it wasn't turned on. "I'm afraid I'm not very good company. I'm still kind of groggy. Can't really think clear."

"Then get some rest. I bought some magazines in the gift shop to entertain myself. I'll just sit quietly here and you let me know if there's anything at all you need, okay?"

"Yeah, thanks." But still he didn't close his eyes. Lisa wondered if he was afraid to. She remembered how she had seen that knife flashing toward her every time she'd closed her eyes Saturday night.

"Would you like to talk about it, Jake?" she asked gently. "I know you must be still reeling from shock right now."

"I don't—" He fell silent, then sighed. "I've known Eric since junior high."

The friend who had died in the crash. "I'm so sorry."

He nodded. "He was a great guy. He and his ex-wife had a couple of boys. He was going to bring them to a race later in the year. He told me he was going to be around after I won the championship at the end of this season to remind me of what a nerd I used to be in high school—just to keep me from getting bigheaded."

And now he had lost both his friend and the chance to win the championship, she thought sadly. "I'm sorry," she said again. "I wish there was something I could say to make you feel better, but I think it's just going to take time for you to heal. In every way."

He heaved another deep sigh. "It would be easier if I could race, rather than sitting around for so long with so much time to think."

Staying busy, focusing on racing. Wade's usual antidote for anything that ailed him, as well. Must be a personality type, she thought, standing to straighten Jake's sheets. She was feeling a little maternal toward him at the moment, even though he was two years her senior.

"You'll be racing again soon enough. Now, try to get some sleep, okay? I'm sure that's what you need most right now."

His eyelids were starting to look heavy again, but he fought it off a little longer. "So, how are things with you and Wade?" he asked drowsily.

She patted his hand, taking care to avoid the IV needle, then returned to her seat. "I'll let you know as soon as I figure that out, myself."

"He's not very good at sharing his feelings."

"That would be an understatement."

His eyes finally closed as he murmured, "Maybe he could get a little better at it—if someone cared enough to help him."

"Someone cares enough," she answered quietly.

His smile was heartbreakingly sad. "I'm glad to hear that. He's a good man. He deserves to be loved."

"He is, Jake."

But Jake was already asleep, the little frown on his face an indication that his dreams weren't happy ones.

"HE JUST SEEMED SO SAD," Lisa mused, sitting in her mother's rose garden with Wade later that evening. "It broke my heart."

"Jake will be okay," Wade assured her gruffly, typically uncomfortable with her emotional wording. "He's lost people before. It never gets any easier, but he'll pull himself together once he's back behind the wheel of his car."

"Racing. The cure for everything that ails you?"

"It is for some of us," he said simply. "Jake, included."

Because she was finally beginning to understand that, she nodded. "Then I hope for his sake that he's back in his car very soon."

"He'll be back the minute he gets clearance from the doctors. And he'll charm them into making that even sooner than they would like."

She smiled. "Jake does have the charm."

Wade frowned at her in the moonlight. "Should I be getting jealous here?"

"No," she assured him with a light laugh. "I seem to be drawn to an entirely different type of charm. A much less obvious type."

Wade looked as though he wasn't sure if he'd just been complimented or insulted, but he let it go.

Lisa sighed and ran a hand through her hair. "The last few weeks, the last few days, in particular, have been crazy. I'm exhausted."

"I won't keep you much longer. I just have one question for you."

Suddenly reenergized, she straightened and turned to look at him. "What question?"

"Are you here to stay this time? Because I'm not sure I can handle it if you take off again."

The unsteadiness in his voice almost undid her. He was trying so hard to be stoic. Working to hide the vulnerabilities he had spent a lifetime denying. Just as it was going to take Jake time to heal from the physical and emotional wounds he had suffered that morning, it was going to take Wade time to learn to fully trust her with his feelings after she had hurt him twice before.

As it happened, they had all the time in the world.

"I'm here to stay," she assured him firmly. "I'll have to go back to Chicago only long enough to pack up my apartment and wrap things up at work, but then I'm coming home. I've already lined up a couple of job interviews within an hour's drive of here, and I'm pretty confident that I can take my pick."

His shoulders seemed to relax a bit. "You want to be close to your parents."

"Yes. And I want to be close to you. Very close, in fact. I'm rather hoping you'll offer me a place to live."

"I just happen to have a fancy motor home and a not-so-fancy, but still quite comfortable house. There's room for you in both of them."

"They sound perfect." She swallowed, then added, "I can't promise to travel with you to every race, Wade. I love my work, but it can be demanding on my time."

"As much as I would like to have you with me every weekend, I can be content knowing you'll be here when

I get back," he returned evenly. "You know how busy I am at the tracks. I don't need a personal cheerleader standing on the sidelines the whole time. And you won't have to worry that I'm looking for any other companionship when you're not there. When I make a commitment, you can take it to the bank."

"I know that."

"I'll be gone a lot, Lees."

She nodded. "As it happens, I'm pretty good at taking care of myself. But I'll go with you when I can. And I'll always be happy to welcome you home."

He lifted her hand to his lips, an uncharacteristically tender gesture that brought a lump to her throat. "I can't always promise to be around when you want me, but I will always been there if you need me," he vowed.

All these years she had told herself that she'd left him because he cared more for racing than for her. When the truth was, she knew now, it had been his inability to express his feelings that had been the real stumbling block for her, leaving her wondering if she would ever really feel important to him.

Blinking back tears, she nodded, making a simple request of her own. "We don't have to be connected at the hip. Just promise me we'll always be connected in our hearts."

"Always. I do love you, you know."

One tear escaped to slide down her cheek. He was trying to express his emotions, she thought. And while he would never be the poetic type, she suspected he would get much better with time and practice. "I love you, too. I always have. I just needed to grow up enough to understand exactly what that means."

He kissed her lingeringly, with a strong hint of the passion that would come as soon as the time was right. Her heart was pounding by the time he finally drew back.

He reached into his shirt pocket. "There's something I've been saving for you."

She watched through a veil of tears as he slipped the diamond ring back into place on her left hand. The horseshoe wasn't the only thing he'd hung onto after she'd left him, apparently. Had he always hoped he'd have a chance to return this to her?

"I won't be giving it back this time," she promised him.

He kissed her again, then rose and held out his hand to her. "Let's go tell your parents. I think your dad's been peeking out the windows for the past twenty minutes."

Laughing, she placed her hand in his, throwing caution to the wind.

* * * * *

Happily ever after is just the beginning....

Turn the page for a sneak preview of
A HEARTBEAT AWAY
by
Eleanor Jones.

*Harlequin Everlasting—Every great love
has a story to tell.* ™
A brand-new series from Harlequin Books

Special? A prickle ran down my neck and my heart started to beat in my ears. Was today really special?

"Tuck in," he ordered.

I turned my attention to the feast that he had spread out on the ground. Thick, home-cooked-ham sandwiches, sausage rolls fresh from the oven and a huge variety of mouthwatering scones and pastries. Hunger pangs took over, and I closed my eyes and bit into soft homemade bread.

When we were finally finished, I lay back against the bluebells with a groan, clutching my stomach.

Daniel laughed. "Your eyes are bigger than your stomach," he told me.

I leaned across to deliver a punch to his arm, but he rolled away, and when my fist met fresh air I collapsed in a fit of giggles before relaxing on my back and staring up into the flawless blue sky. We lay like that for quite a while, Daniel and I, side by side in companionable silence, until he stretched out his hand in an arc that encompassed the whole area.

"Don't you think that this is the most beautiful place in the entire world?"

His voice held a passion that echoed my own feelings, and I rose onto my elbow and picked a buttercup to hide the emotion that clogged my throat.

"Roll over onto your back," I urged, prodding him with my forefinger. He obliged with a broad grin, and I reached across to place the yellow flower beneath his chin.

"Now, let us see if you like butter."

When a yellow light shone on the tanned skin below his jaw, I laughed.

"There…you do."

For an instant our eyes met and I had the strangest sense that I was drowning in those honey-brown depths. The scent of bluebells engulfed me. A roaring filled my ears, and then, unexpectedly, in one smooth movement Daniel rolled me onto my back and plucked a buttercup of his own.

"And do *you* like butter, Lucy McTavish?" he asked. When he placed the flower against my skin, time stood still.

His long lean body was suspended over mine, pinning me against the grass. Daniel…dear, comfortable, familiar Daniel was suddenly bringing out in me the strangest sensations.

"Do you, Lucy McTavish?" he asked again, his voice low and vibrant.

My eyes flickered toward his, the whisper of a sigh escaped my lips and although a strange lethargy had crept into my limbs, I somehow felt as if all my nerve endings were on fire. He felt it, too—I could see it in his warm brown eyes. And when he lowered his face to mine, it seemed to me the most natural thing in the world.

None of the kisses I had ever experienced could have even begun to prepare me for the feel of Daniel's lips on mine. My entire body floated on a tide of ecstasy that shut out everything but his soft, warm mouth, and I knew that this was what I had been waiting for the whole of my life.

"Oh, Lucy." He pulled away to look into my eyes. "Why haven't we done this before?"

Holding his gaze, I gently touched his cheek, then I curled my fingers through the short thick hair at the base of his skull, overwhelmed by the longing to drown again in the sensations that flooded our bodies. And when his long tanned fingers crept across my tingling skin, I knew I could deny him nothing.

* * * * *

Be sure to look for
A HEARTBEAT AWAY,
available February 27, 2007.

And look, too, for
THE DEPTH OF LOVE
by Margot Early,
the story of a couple who must learn
that love comes in many guises—
and in the end it's the only thing that counts.

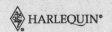

REQUEST YOUR FREE BOOKS!
2 FREE NOVELS PLUS 2 FREE GIFTS!

Silhouette®

SPECIAL EDITION®

Life, Love and Family!

YES! Please send me 2 FREE Silhouette Special Edition® novels and my 2 FREE gifts. After receiving them, if I don't wish to receive any more books, I can return the shipping statement marked "cancel." If I don't cancel, I will receive 6 brand-new novels every month and be billed just $4.24 per book in the U.S., or $4.99 per book in Canada, plus 25¢ shipping and handling per book and applicable taxes, if any*. That's a savings of at least 15% off the cover price! I understand that accepting the 2 free books and gifts places me under no obligation to buy anything. I can always return a shipment and cancel at any time. Even if I never buy another book from Silhouette, the two free books and gifts are mine to keep forever. 235 SDN EEYU 335 SDN EEY6

Name	(PLEASE PRINT)	
Address		Apt.
City	State/Prov.	Zip/Postal Code

Signature (if under 18, a parent or guardian must sign)

Mail to the Silhouette Reader Service™:
IN U.S.A.: P.O. Box 1867, Buffalo, NY 14240-1867
IN CANADA: P.O. Box 609, Fort Erie, Ontario L2A 5X3

Not valid to current Silhouette Special Edition subscribers.

Want to try two free books from another line?
Call 1-800-873-8635 or visit www.morefreebooks.com.

* Terms and prices subject to change without notice. NY residents add applicable sales tax. Canadian residents will be charged applicable provincial taxes and GST. This offer is limited to one order per household. All orders subject to approval. Credit or debit balances in a customer's account(s) may be offset by any other outstanding balance owed by or to the customer. Please allow 4 to 6 weeks for delivery.

Your Privacy: Silhouette is committed to protecting your privacy. Our Privacy Policy is available online at www.eHarlequin.com or upon request from the Reader Service. From time to time we make our lists of customers available to reputable firms who may have a product or service of interest to you. If you would prefer we not share your name and address, please check here. ☐

SSE07

Hearts racing
Blood pumping
Pulses accelerating

Falling in love can be a blur…especially at
180 mph!

So if you crave the thrill of the chase—on and off the track—you'll love

SPEED BUMPS
by Ken Casper!

On sale May 2007

www.GetYourHeartRacing.com

Hearts racing
Blood pumping
Pulses accelerating

Falling in love can be a blur…especially at
180 mph!

So if you crave the thrill of the chase—on and off the track—you'll love

SPEED BUMPS
by Ken Casper!

On sale May 2007

www.GetYourHeartRacing.com